Taking Down a Boss

Taking Down a Boss

Shmel Carter

www.urbanbooks.net

Urban Books, LLC
300 Farmingdale Road, N.Y.-Route 109
Farmingdale, NY 11735

ISBN 13: 978-1-64556-379-2
ISBN 10: 1-64556-379-0

First Trade Paperback Printing December 2022
Printed in the United States of America

10 9 8 7 6 5 4 3 2 1

This is a work of fiction. Any references or similarities to actual events, real people, living or dead, or to real locales are intended to give the novel a sense of reality. Any similarity in other names, characters, places, and incidents is entirely coincidental.

Distributed by Kensington Publishing Corp.
Submit Orders to:
Customer Service
400 Hahn Road
Westminster, MD 21157-4627
Phone: 1-800-733-3000
Fax: 1-800-659-2436

Taking Down a Boss

Dedication

This book is dedicated to the matriarch of my family,
Dorothy Walker, my grandma. You hold everyone down.
I love you with everything in me.
Lennie F. Mickey
It broke my heart when I found out you were gone.
I knew something was wrong when I couldn't reach you
on the phone.
I was not prepared for this. Mickey, why did you have to
die?
I was at a loss for words. All I could do was cry.
You were my friend, and we had plans.
God, please, help me to understand. No, he was not
perfect, but he was a good man.
No one can replace the memories we share.
No matter what went on, you always showed me you
cared.
I miss you, and I must accept the fact that you are gone.
I promise you one thing: through me, your legacy will
continue to live on.
I miss you.
May you RIP.
Sunrise, January 27, 1977
Sunset, January 7, 2016

Acknowledgments

First, I want to give honor to God. Without him, I would not be where I am today. To my fans, thank you for your continuous support. George S. Hudson (G), thank you again for this opportunity. Raquel Williams, thank you for letting me be a part of your team. The girls keep me rolling in the chat room. I may not say much, but they help me get through my day.

Shona Robinson, I would like to thank you as well. I am so proud of you and Amir. You are doing big things. I pray the Bullies Bar and Grill will be an immense success. I will always support you in all you do, just like you do me. Tempis J., Brie Tolbert, and Quisha Dynae, I swear y'all keep me laughing in the chat room. Thank you for that extra push. The Lord knows I needed some motivation. I had nothing in me to write. I was going through so much.

My nephew, Cameron Frazier, you did it. West Charlotte Senior High School Class of 2016. Your journey to NC A&T has just begun. Aggie Pride. I am a proud auntie. My other nephew, Darius Walker Junior, I am proud to say that you are on your way. You are growing more and more each day. You finally got it. It doesn't matter how long it took. I am happy that you got it. My niece, Hailey Smith, I am so proud of you too. South Mecklenburg Class of 2016. This world ain't ready for you, baby doll.

Congratulations to my cousin, Crystal Davis, now Mrs. White. I am so happy for you. You deserve it. Cathey

Johnson, our time is coming. Marnita Bell Kilgo, thank you for listening to me vent. God knows I needed those motherly talks. I thank you even more because the talks always stayed between us. Thank you for all your motherly advice and for never choosing sides between us. For that, you are the real MVP. Sybrina Massey, I must thank you as well. I thank God for our bond. My firstborn, A. 'Yana Hughes. You are about to embark on your last year of high school. I am still in shock. The odds were stacked against you before you were even born. We showed the world that my life was not over when I became pregnant with you. I was a scared teenager and didn't know what to do. Look at you now. As long as you make it, I make it too. Erica Hughes, your journey has just begun. I don't think high school is ready for you. Ready or not, here you come. Eric Hughes Junior, my baby and only son. You came out fighting for your life. All I heard was you were not breathing. Guess what? I was not even worried. The God I serve had you the whole time. You are still fighting for your life. I stressed for months about the title of this book. Once you heard my plot, you came up with the name *The Setup*, even though I changed it midway through the book. I thank you for that, son. I love you.

Gloria McKinney, I did not birth you, but I love you like I did. This is your last year in high school. I want you to embrace it. Take this world by storm because they ain't ready for my glowworm. Kayla Harris, I have enjoyed getting to know you and watching you blossom into a beautiful young lady. Valencia Frazier, I love having you as my big sister. If I left anyone out, charge it to my mind and not my heart. I love y'all.

This letter is in remembrance of my daddy

I remember calling you on the phone because I had missed curfew. I was crying because you didn't play, so I didn't know what to do. I remember the first dude to ever step to you. You looked him in the face and told him he was bold. You didn't play about me, and I was only 16 years old.

I remember talking to you about my first heartbreak. You held me in your arms and said, "Baby, it's going to be okay."

I remember calling to tell you I was pregnant and please not be mad. You told me you had my back because you were still my dad. Of course, you were all I had.

I remember that smile on your face when you came to visit me at Shaw University. You told me you loved me as we embraced.

I remember you were eating your favorite meal the night before you died. A few hours later, the news I received was so unreal. Your world was over. My daddy was gone. All I kept hearing my cousin say was they couldn't get me on the phone. My life has not been the same since you left this world. I find comfort in knowing you are watching over your baby girl. I love and miss you, Dad. You are the one person that never judged me. You always told me when I was wrong and made sure I knew it, but you had my back—right or wrong. Nobody can ever replace my daddy. You were a real father. You stepped up to the plate and raised me. You were not a weekend dad. I don't know where I would be now if you hadn't gotten me out of my situation and raised me. I want to thank you for loving me. Yarvin Carter, may you RIP.

Chapter 1

Keena and Kim

Pop! Pop! Pow! That was all I heard as I was running for cover. Every time I turned around, Kim got me in some shit. I mean, damn. I saw her bobbing and weaving through the cars. I watched as Bone, the local drug dealer, chased her. I was waiting for the perfect time to take his ass up out of here. I could not let him continue to breathe. I was always taught if you try to kill somebody, make sure your target is dead. I knew if I didn't, he was sure to come after us.

Hi, I'm Keena, and this crazy bitch bobbing and weaving is my girl, Kim. We are known for getting with niggas and setting their asses up to be robbed, and we were good at it. Of course, we were the only two that knew that besides one other person. We could never let that secret get out because it would make our job harder . . . or we could get killed. Niggas would be waiting on us. I don't know how Kim let this nigga end up with the gun, but lately, she has been slipping.

I watched him as he stopped to catch his breath. He looked around. I knew he was looking for Kim but didn't have a clue where she was. That was my time to light up his ass. *Pow!* I saw his head explode after I shot his ass dead in the middle of his forehead with my 9 mm. I *never* missed my mark. My daddy kept me on the shooting range when I was younger. I saw all the blood rushing out of his head as he slowly sank to the ground.

Now, the nosy neighbors were starting to come out of their houses. I refuse to go to jail for killing this low-life nigga. Even though we were in the hood, I knew we had to leave the scene like right now because I didn't want to be around when twelve got here. Twelve is the police, just in case you didn't know.

When I hopped in the little hooptie that I kept around for jobs like this, Kim jumped into the passenger seat. She better be glad she came when she did because I would have hated to leave her. Deep down, I knew I would never have left her, though, because Kim is my girl.

"Damn, I thought that nigga was going to kill me. What took you so damn long?"

I looked at that bitch out of the corner of my eye as sweat was dripping down the side of her face, and her mouth was twitching. I just shook my head at her. I mean, she left me speechless for a moment. I had to take a second to breathe before I let loose on her ass. This dumb bitch didn't have a clue. I couldn't believe she fixed her mouth to say that shit to me.

"What the hell you mean what took me so long? That nigga should have never even left the damn house. You were supposed to smoke that fool. Why did *I* have to kill his ass? I'm getting a bigger cut. How much did you get anyway?" I was asking question after question as she looked at me all funny. Hell, I didn't care. "What?" I asked her. I didn't even give her a chance to answer as I snatched the duffle bag from her lap. I stuck my tongue out at her as I unzipped the bag while I drove down West Boulevard.

"Damn, bitch." I high-fived her. First, I saw at least two bricks of cocaine in the bag. I hadn't even seen the money yet because I was already mentally counting the money from the dope. I knew I could quickly sell that to Joc. He loved buying his dope from me. Hell, I never taxed his ass, so he was getting superior quality dope at a cheap price. I only charged him thirty thousand apiece. I easily could have gotten at least thirty-five or thirty-six thousand. It didn't matter to me, though. I was not a dope dealer. I knew my shit, though, from watching my daddy. I always thought like a nigga, so they could never get over on me. Hell, I was getting the dope for free anyway. Either way, it was a profit when I didn't have to pay for it. Just from the two bricks that was already thirty thousand apiece for each of us. I finally looked at the money. Just from a quick scanning, it looked like about fifty thousand. I was not expecting this much from Bone. I thought he was a nickel-and-dime hustler. I guess I thought wrong.

Chapter 2

Keena

I pulled into the Vue Apartments in downtown Charlotte, North Carolina. I have a two-bedroom-plus-a-den condo on the fifth floor. I pay $2,800 a month to stay here. Hell, this shit ain't cheap. But my living room view overlooks Bearden Park, home of the Charlotte Knights. Now, you can see why I do what I do. Fuck getting a job. This *is* my job. I cannot see myself working no damn body's nine to five. I would go crazy listening to somebody trying to tell me what to do all day, every day. I have been supporting myself for a long time, but I ain't never had a job. Hell, a regular job cannot afford my lifestyle anyway.

I thought back to the day when my dad got killed. It seemed like just a typical day. I remember it like it was yesterday.

I was only 13 when my father got killed. That was also the day I caught my first body. One of the niggas got away, but I never forget a face. He shot my daddy in cold blood. I have been looking for him for a long time. I don't care how long it will take to find him because when I do, I will kill him.

I was watching TV with my dad when our silent alarm went off. He reached for the remote and flicked the TV to the cameras he had throughout the house. My dad was a kingpin. He did not trust anybody and taught me never to trust anybody. Then the lights started flickering before they went out completely. The house was completely dark. I did not even realize my daddy had gotten up off the bed, but I saw the red beam from my daddy's gun on the head of one of the robbers. That robber had a hole in the middle of his forehead before I could even blink my eyes.

The next thing I knew, I felt the whole room shake. My eyes were starting to burn. I took the scarf I had been wearing on my head and placed it on my face. I later found out that it was tear gas. My eyes had adjusted to the dark by this time as I looked around the room to see what was happening. I swiftly grabbed the gun off the dead robber. I felt the wetness on my hand as I made my way toward my mark. Without even seeing what it was, I knew it was blood. The rust scent of it was so strong.

Out of the corner of my eye, I saw the other robber trying to sneak up on my daddy. Just as he looked over at me, I shot him in the middle of his forehead, just like my dad had trained me to do. Dad had been grooming me my whole life for this. I never thought it would come this soon, but my daddy never lied to me. When I was old enough to ask him what he did, he told me the truth. He said he was a drug dealer. He already knew I would hear it in the streets, so he wanted to be the one to tell me.

I was my daddy's only child. He spoiled me rotten, and he treated me like a princess. I was just 2 years old when my dad took me from my mom. She was so jealous of me that she would beat me until I turned colors. Then she would keep me from him until my bruises healed.

My daddy didn't want her anymore, so she took it out on me. That was sad. A grown-ass woman jealous of a child.

She had me kidnapped when I was 10 years old, trying to extort some money out of him. She knew he would pay to get me back. The whole city knew Jake didn't play about me. Her plan didn't work, though. I already told y'all my daddy was a kingpin. He already knew she had me. The streets belonged to him. He knew everything that went on in the streets of Charlotte. Nothing went on in this city without him knowing about it. I don't understand why she thought her plan would work.

My mom was dumb for even thinking that my father, Jake, would let her continue to breathe after that. I watched my daddy shoot her between her eyes. I didn't even cry when she died. My daddy even took me to the funeral like everything was OK. I felt no remorse for the woman that brought me into this world. That was a sad thought because a child is supposed to have a love for their mom. She held me captive for three days when she kidnapped me and tortured me the whole time. She acted like she never birthed me, like I was a stranger. That bitch wouldn't even feed me. Now, that was some fuck shit right there, the way she treated me, so fuck her. I hope that bitch was rotting in hell.

Kim snapped me out of my daydream.

"Damn, bitch. What are you thinking about?"

"Nothing. Let me see that bag." Kim knew I was lying because she knew me better than I knew myself at times. We had been friends too long for me to try to tell her nothing was bothering me when it really was.

I pulled out all the money from the bag and ran it through my money machine. It ended up being exactly $80,000. I handed Kim her forty thousand and picked up my phone to call Joc. He answered on the first ring, just like I knew he would. He always anticipated my phone calls.

"What do it do, Keena? You got something for me?"

"You already know I do, Joc. Same place, same time."

"All right; bet." We hung up.

My next call was to my white girl, Becky. She washed up all my dirty money for me. I had a bunch of Laundromats and real estate around the city. She even had me invested in a few nightclubs as a silent partner. Money was not an issue for me. Thanks to Becky, I also had a few investments in stocks and bonds. I didn't want to keep living this lifestyle. Eventually, I wanted to settle down and have some kids.

"Hey, Keena. What you been up to?"

"You know me, Becky. Same thang, different day."

"Yes, I know," she said with a light chuckle.

"I'll be by the bank tomorrow."

"OK, I got you." We hung up. I looked over at Kim. She had dozed off, and some drool dribbled down her face. I was starting to worry about her. She was really slacking. I didn't know what her problem was, but I would find the underlying cause before she got me killed. I didn't even like doing robberies in Charlotte. We lay our heads there, and I wasn't planning on moving out of the city, so I knew that was a dumb move. You don't shit where you sleep. Hell, Charlotte was not that damn big. Everybody knew every damn body. Kim was well known because she stayed on the party scene, but I let her talk me into robbing Bone—against my better judgment. Then she almost got herself killed. Not to mention *I* could have gotten killed as well. This would be our first—and last—

robbery in Charlotte. I had been planning all the licks. I was always the brain. For real, I could probably do it by myself, but I wanted her to get paid too. I don't know why I let *her* plan this one. I left Kim asleep on my sofa as I headed out to meet Joc.

I hopped in my 2015 smoky-gray 745 BMW and sped off through the city. This car right here was my baby. My daddy had one, so that was how I was introduced to it. I whipped my Beamer to Orange Street in Grier Heights. Joc had a dope house over there. I drove my Beamer because I had secret compartments built all through it. My white girl, Becky, had put me on the dude she was messing with that customized cars. This was the best investment I ever made. If I got pulled over, the police dogs could not detect my shit. I had coffee grinds all in my secret compartment. Coffee grinds always threw off a dog's nose.

Joc was standing in the doorway with his shirt off when I pulled into the driveway. I looked at him as he licked his sexy-ass LL Cool J lips. He was drinking a bottle of Fiji water. I had to catch myself as I watched him. I was dreaming about me sucking that water off his lips. Joc was sexy as hell. I was secretly crushing on him. He had a bald head with an AK tatted on his neck. He was not fat, but he was thick. He was about two twenty solid. His pecan-tan complexion and oh, his smile . . . His smile was bright as he showed off those pearly whites. He could do a toothpaste commercial. I always had a lot of confidence in myself, but not when it came to him. Joc made me lose all sense of direction. He never knew it, though.

I parked my car and waited for him to get in it.

"What do I owe you, Keena?"

"Well, I got two of them thangs, so sixty thousand."

"OK. Hold on. I'll be right back."

I watched him as he got out of the car. Damn, that nigga knows he's sexy. Women be flocking to him because he got money. Everybody knows even the ugliest niggas could get the baddest women if they had money. His looks ain't bad, *and* he got money. He didn't pay the women any attention, though. I didn't see him entertain too many women. I thought he was gay when I first started coming around him. My smart-ass mouth had to ask him. He laughed at me. He told me he has never been a male whore. He's a man and has sex, but he was looking for the right one. Eventually, he wanted out of the streets too.

I snapped out of my trance when he slid back into my passenger seat and handed me my money.

"I gave you seventy instead of sixty, Keena."

"That's what's up, Joc. Why did you do that, though? I only charge you thirty. Hell, I get them for free."

"I know you do, but I wanted to. Keena, can I ask you something?"

"You already know you can." I turned in my seat to give him my undivided attention.

"Are you tired of your lifestyle?"

I thought about what he said for a moment before I spoke. "I *am* tired, but I ain't ready to stop. I want to be financially set. I don't like depending on nobody. Kim and I met in a group home. We grew up with nothing. I was 2 years old when my mom started beating me. My dad immediately took me from her when he found out. I was 13 when my dad got killed right in front of me. I had a good life before my dad died, but nobody in my family wanted to keep me, so I was shipped off to the group home. Kim watched her mom's boyfriend kill her. Then she was shipped off to a group home around the same time I was. She was my first friend. It has always been us and nobody else. My A1 since Day 1."

"Wow, I didn't know that."

"Nobody really knows. I don't let too many people into my world too quick."

"Well, you let me in."

"I know I did. I feel comfortable talking to you."

"Let me take you out, Keena. I know you're feeling a brother. I be seeing you looking at me." He started laughing. "Don't think I don't be checking you out."

I was trying to hide the way I was feeling. I didn't want to seem too anxious. "Joc, let me take a rain check." I could see the look of disappointment on his face.

"It ain't what you're thinking, Joc. I like you, but I'm headed out of town. I'm not sure how long I'll be gone, so I don't want to start nothing until I get back."

"You going to hit that lick that I put you on?"

"Yes, I am. I had to study that nigga first, though. I think it's time now, but I want to come back alive," I told him with a chuckle.

"A'ight, ma. Be easy. That sounds fair." He got out of the car. It took everything in me to turn him down. I was feeling the fuck out of him. I ain't never had any sex. I know what y'all be thinking. I set up those niggas. They be so damn horny they be thinking they're going to get some ass. Then I be in and out before they even knew what hit them. I looked at Joc one last time before I drove off.

Chapter 3

Kim

I woke up, and Keena was gone. I didn't know where the hell she had run off to. To be perfectly honest, I didn't even really care. I looked around her apartment. It was nice, just like mine used to be. I never let her come over to my spot anymore because I was too embarrassed. I was starting to let myself go. Keena didn't know it, but I needed this money bad as hell. I was broke. I was putting all my money up my nose. And now, I was starting to hate my own friend, and she hadn't even done anything to me. The drugs were taking over my thought processes. I was becoming jealous of her, and I shouldn't have been. I knew that as long as Keena had it, I had it too.

Keena loved me unconditionally, but I had started selling all my shit just to get high. Now, I was about to lose my condo. I owed my mortgage company $12,000. I was going to use this money to catch up on my mortgage. I also was behind three months on my car payment. Most of my money was already gone. I was so high today that I almost got not only Keena but also myself killed. That would have never happened if I was not high. I was usually on my shit. Then Keena had the nerve to say she was getting a bigger cut. I thank God she played fair because I was going to kill her ass today. I didn't want to, but the way I was hurting for money, my greed would have overshadowed my thought processes.

I thought back to the day I met Bone. Yes, Bone. This lick we just did was personal to me. Keena didn't want to go out that night, so I decided to go to Club Label by myself. That was one of the worst decisions I ever made in my life. I was at the bar getting ready to buy myself a drink when he walked up and introduced himself.

"Hey, sexy. What are you drinking?"

"Pineapple juice and vodka," I told him. He waved the bartender over and told him to put my drink on his tab.

"Wow, big spender," I said jokingly.

"Yes, there is more where that came from. You gotta come over to the winning team."

"The winning team, huh?" I said playfully back to him.

I talked and danced with him all night. I even did something I never do. I let Bone go to the bar and buy me another drink without me going with him. That time, he dropped a Mickey into my glass. My life has been spiraling downhill ever since then. That night, I fucked the shit out of Bone. I was not in my right mind. I don't even get down like that. He also introduced me to cocaine. I never told Keena about Bone, but I should have. I wouldn't be in the situation I'm in now if I had confided in my best friend, but I was too embarrassed. I couldn't let this nigga live after what he did to me. We don't even rob niggas from Charlotte. It's too close to home, but he had to pay. Ever since, I've been searching high and low for that high, but I can't find it. I have always heard there is nothing like that first high.

I made my way to the kitchen. I was hungry as hell. I knew Keena had some food. We both knew how to cook. I didn't really feel like cooking, so I threw a pizza in the oven.

While waiting for my pizza, I turned on the sixty-inch smart TV. I hadn't watched TV in a while because I had sold all of mine. I was going to cop me one today, though.

I hope Keena has a job lined up. Then I would be broke again after I caught up on everything.

I flipped the channels on the TV until I landed on *Power*. Everybody was talking about it, but I hadn't had a chance to watch it. I knew Keena better than she knew herself and vice versa. I knew she had recorded all the episodes. I went into the kitchen to get my pizza and grabbed a can of Sunkist. I wanted to be comfortable.

I was in the middle of episode two, season one, when Keena walked in the door.

"What you doing, bitch?" she asked me as she walked toward her couch and flopped down.

"Not shit. Trying to catch up on *Power*."

"Catch up? You ain't been watching this shit? Girl, this show is addictive. I love me some Ghost. That wife of his, Tasha, oh yeah, that bitch the truth. She be on some gangster shit." She scooted closer to me. It reminded me of our group home days. Whenever Keena had a nightmare about her father's murder, she would climb in bed with me. I would always massage her head and let her know it was all right.

"Kim, let's go shopping. I want to go to South Park Mall and fuck up some commas." She flopped back on her butter-soft, all-white couch. I didn't have the money to fuck up some commas with her, even though I wanted to.

"Not today, Keena. I'll take a rain check." She just stared at me. She knew I liked to shop. It didn't matter how I felt. Shopping was always my therapy. I just knew if I went, I would blow at least five thousand in the mall, and I couldn't afford to do that right now. I had too many bills to catch up on.

"Well, let's go get pampered then. We deserve a pedicure. You need your raggedy-ass sew-in done over again." She was laughing, but I knew she was serious. We made a vow to each other years ago to keep each other on point.

"What are you holding back for? We got plenty of money, Kim. We gotta spoil ourselves. Who else is going to do it?"

I wanted to scream, "Correction, bitch, *you* got plenty of money to spend." She didn't know my money was funny. But I knew I had to do something to get her off my back.

"Let's go get our feet done. I'll worry about my hair later. I ain't going nowhere." I jumped off the couch to grab my $500 Coach Hobo bag off the counter. I remember when going into the store to get this was nothing to me. I definitely had to get my shit together.

Chapter 4

Keena

I noticed how Kim didn't want to go shopping. I hope she don't think I ain't paying her no attention. That is my sister from another mister. I love this girl, and something is going on with her. I already knew it was a money issue. I guess she forgot I was her emergency contact on everything. I knew her car payment was behind. What I didn't know was *why* it was behind. We never walked away with less than forty thousand apiece from each lick. Her appearance was starting to change as well. I was going to find the underlying cause of this.

"Oh, before I forget, Kim." I reached into my pocketbook and handed her the thirty-five thousand, which was her cut from the dope I sold Joc. I saw her exhale a little bit.

"Girl, Joc asked me out."

"So, bitch, where are you going?"

"I told him I would take a rain check."

"You did *what?* Why would you do that? You know you like that nigga. You need some dick in your life. What are you waiting on?"

"I like him, but I didn't want to seem too eager. I hope I didn't fuck up."

The first store I hit when we walked into the mall was Coach. I loved that store. I picked up a pair of Urban

Hiker boots. They were the tan color I was looking for. I also picked up a pair of loafers and a pair of red Coach tennis shoes. I dropped over a thousand dollars in that store. I noticed Kim was not really buying anything.

"What's wrong with you, bitch?"

"Nothing. You said we would get our toes done, not shop."

"We *are* going to get them done, but I wanted to spend some time with my bestie. You don't want nothing?"

"No, not out of here."

The next store we hit up was Bath and Body Works. Now, if Kim didn't buy anything out of here, I *knew* something was up. They had a huge sale going on, which was nothing new. They had a five for eighteen dollars or a seven for twenty-four dollars. They also had the wallflowers on sale. I needed some more of those as well. We both ended up spending over $200 in that store.

I was exhausted when we made it to the nail shop. I stuck my feet in the water and relaxed my head back as I let the Chinese people do what they do best.

"I'm hungry, Kim. Where do you want to eat?"

"It doesn't really matter to me. I'm down for whatever."

"Cheesecake Factory it is then."

While I was waiting on my food, my text alert went off. My face lit up when I saw who it was from. Joc had sent me a text message.

Joc: I'm still waiting on my rain check.

Me: I got you, Joc.

He sent back a bunch of hugs and kisses emoji.

"What you over there grinning so hard for?"

"Joc just sent me a text message saying he was waiting to cash in his rain check."

"I don't know why you keep playing with that man. He wants you just as bad as you want him."

"I know. I just don't want to seem too eager. He has all kinds of women flocking to him."

"Well, he wants *you.*"

I nodded my head.

I was thinking about Joc and Kim's words as I ate my food. I ain't never been in a relationship before. My dad set the bar high. Any nigga I dealt with had to come correct or don't come at all. Truth be told, I was a virgin. I was a 24-year-old virgin. I was just waiting on the right one. I ain't saying we had to be married. I just wanted something real.

"Will these be separate tickets?" the waitress asked us.

"Put it on one ticket. It's my treat."

"Well, thanks, bestie."

Afterward, I dropped Kim off at home and headed to my place.

Chapter 5

Kim

I was happy that Keena didn't want to come in. I didn't know how I would explain my living situation to her. I walked into my house and was disgusted. Powder residue was all over my kitchen table. I knew I had to clean up. My place was nasty. I usually don't play like that. I can't stand a nasty-ass house or a nasty bitch. I was starting to become what I despised. I went into my laundry room and grabbed my cleaning supplies. Then I sprayed bleach and Fabuloso everywhere. I got out some gloves and scrubbed the condo down. I was satisfied with the result. I knew I needed some help kicking this cocaine addiction, and I knew Keena wouldn't judge me, but I was too ashamed.

I picked up my phone to call my girl, Nina. She was a beast with her sew-ins. I knew if I paid her double, she would come tonight. We had gotten our feet done, but not our nails. Nina said she would be right over. Only a few people knew where I lay my head, and she was one of them. I knew we would be hitting the road soon for another lick. I had to be looking my best. Nina said to give her a few hours, and she would be here. That gave me plenty of time to run to Walmart and grab a TV.

I was browsing the electronic section when I heard a sexy voice. His voice was so deep that I felt my panties get wet. I turned around to match the face with the voice. He was sexy as fuck.

"You need some help, ma?"

"Not unless you work here," I said as I moved my hand around to gesture around the store. He started laughing at me.

"Do I look like I work here?" He didn't look like he worked at Walmart. He had on a pair of Levi's and a polo shirt. On his feet, he wore Retro 13s. His wrist was iced out. He had on a Ferragamo watch with diamonds throughout the face. I knew that watch was at least $2,000. He also had on a yellow gold pinky ring. That ring was blinged out too. He was mocha chocolate, and he stood about six-two.

"Nah, you don't look like you work here. I am kind of in a hurry, though." I tried to walk around him. Nina will be at my house soon. I needed to get the TV hooked up. He gently grabbed my arm.

"What's your name, ma? A nigga is trying to get to know you."

"Kim."

"Well, Ms. Kim, do you have a number? I know you do. Your phone is in your hand." He was pointing with a smirk on his face.

"Just because I have a phone don't mean I want *you* to have the number," I said while smiling the whole time.

"Quit playing, Kim," he said as he placed his phone in my hand. He wanted me to put my number on his phone. So I did and handed him back his phone.

"You never told me your name."

"My name is Ashton."

"Hmm, Ashton. I like that, even though you don't look like an Ashton."

He started laughing. "What does an Ashton look like?"

"I don't know. It's a white boy's name."

"I'm going to call you tonight, Kim. Don't be playing with a nigga." I just looked back at him and laughed as I walked off.

I had just finished getting my TVs set up when I heard the doorbell ring. I bought two TVs—one for my den, and the other for my bedroom. Nina's my girl and all, but she loves to run her mouth. That bitch wouldn't get the chance to say anything about me. We are *not* friend friends. We are *just* associates. She ain't Keena.

"Hey, girl."

She greeted me when I opened my door, then reached out and hugged me. "Damn, Kim. You should have called me last week. What the hell is going on with your hair?"

I put my hand up to my hair. I didn't think it looked that bad. Compared to what she was used to seeing, I guess it did.

We caught up on all the gossip while she was doing my hair. When she was done, she stuck her mirror in my face. She had my shit laid. I couldn't complain. I handed her $250 and sent her on out the door. Then I ran to my room because I heard my phone ringing. It was Keena.

"What's up, bitch?" I answered, out of breath.

"Damn, bitch. Did I catch you at a bad time? You sound like you're fucking," she said, laughing.

"Nah, bitch, because if I was fucking, we wouldn't be talking," I jokingly replied. "I was letting Nina out the door and heard my phone, so I ran to it."

"Oh, it's about damn time you did something to your head. How are we supposed to catch ballers if we ain't looking like we belong to one?" I didn't say anything. I knew she was right. I had to get back on my game. This is how I ate.

"I know, Keena. What's up? I know you didn't call me to talk about my hair."

"We're leaving for Miami tomorrow. I been watching this nigga name Peter for a while now. Joc put me on this lick. All he wants is his connect information out of the deal. They call this nigga Black. We gonna be out there for a while. He doesn't trust anybody. His last girlfriend was killed on the campus of Florida A&M. I don't know all the details. All I know is that she was killed, and that was the only girlfriend he ever had. We can retire off this one if we play it right. I'm tired of this lifestyle. I want to get married and have a bunch of babies."

I started laughing.

"You want to do *what?*"

"Bitch, you heard me. Shit, this toy ain't doing it for me no more. I want some dick."

"You ain't never had none. How you know that's what you want?"

"Well, I damn sure don't want no pussy."

"That ain't what I'm saying, Keena. I'm just saying you can't miss what you ain't never had."

"True."

"I'll see you tomorrow." We hung up.

Chapter 6

Keena

I hung up the phone with Kim and started packing my bags. I hope Kim brought her A-game. I been watching this nigga for two years. I couldn't afford no fuckups. I knew it was going to be hard to get next to him. He didn't like clingy, loudmouthed women. I knew everything about him. I knew his favorite color, which was green. His favorite food was Italian. I even knew every Sunday, he ate dinner with his mom and sister. He took care of them. His father was killed when he was younger, just like mine. His mom was pregnant with his sister when his dad was killed. She never met him. That was thirteen years ago. He was 14 when it happened and was now 27.

His birthday was on April eleventh, which was around the corner. I knew he was having a big birthday party at a club called Mansion. He spent a lot of money on this party. Jay-Z and T.I. were going to be in the building, along with a host of other celebrities. That's why it was now or never. He didn't believe in just coincidence running into someone. So it was important that we be at this party. He also donated to the Juvenile Diabetes Foundation yearly because his sister had it. I grabbed my iPad to look up some flights. One was leaving tomorrow at two in the afternoon. I booked the flight for both of us. Then I looked up hotels. I found one on Brickell Avenue.

It was the Four Seasons Hotel. It was $349 a night, a little steep because I don't believe in wasting money just because I had it. But I could afford it. I had over $500,000 in my bank account. I knew in order to attract money, you had to look like money.

I sent Kim a text message letting her know all the information about our trip. She responded, telling me she was cool with what I had done. Then I decided to send Joc a text message. I needed somebody to know where we were staying at just . . . in case. He called instead of texting back. I was blushing as I answered the phone.

"What's up, sexy?"

"Not much. I was informing you where I'll be staying once I get to Miami."

"Thanks for telling me. Be careful, Keena. I be worried about you."

"Really?"

"Why wouldn't I? I mean, I do business with you, but you know I been feeling you."

"Yes, I know."

"Think about what I said, Keena. You don't have to keep doing this. I'll take care of you."

"It ain't about the money. When I come back, you can take me out."

"You promise?" I could hear the smile in his voice.

"Yes, I do. I'm feeling you too." I couldn't believe I had admitted it.

"How long are you going to be in Miami?"

"I'm not sure. The only thing I *am* sure of is this is my last lick."

"That's music to my ears. I'm happy to hear that. Call me if you need me. I'll be on the next plane."

"I will."

"I mean it, Keena."

We hung up. I knew I had to get up early. I had shit to do in the morning. I also had to get a manicure, but I didn't have to worry about my hair because my weave was already tight.

The next morning, I woke up bright and early. I ran into Walmart to holla at my girl, Sue. She does nails there. She's the only one I have let touch my hands for the past five years.

After leaving there, I ran to the bank to drop my money off to Becky. I needed her to handle that for me.

I wanted to see Joc before I left. I shot him a text message. I was sitting in the bank parking lot waiting on him to return my text.

Joc: You know where I'm at, ma.

Me: I'm on my way.

That was all I needed to hear. I headed to Grier Heights. I really did like Joc. We've been flirting with each other for three years.

Joc was waiting on me when I pulled up. He looked good in his Gucci jeans along with his red and black Gucci shirt and matching belt. He wore a pair of black Air Force Ones. He even had on a black Gucci hat. I looked him up and down as he walked over to my car and opened the door. Then I got out of the vehicle.

He stepped back and looked at me.

"Damn, ma. You look good. Don't have me come to Miami and catch a case."

I turned all the way around so that he could get a better look. I wore a blue jean Anne Klein dress with a pair of six-inch red Steve Madden heels. He was my favorite shoe designer. Joc grabbed me and hugged me, and I hugged him back. Then he kissed me on my neck before he let me go. My pussy instantly got wet. Joc may just be the one to get my virginity.

"I had to see you before I left. I can't explain my reasons."

"You don't need an excuse to see me, ma." I looked him in his eyes. I knew what he said was genuine.

"When you come back, I got you." He hugged me again. Then I got into my car and drove off.

Chapter 7

Kim

I was waiting for Keena to come pick me up so we could head to the airport. She said we could retire after this, but I knew I couldn't. Keena had a nice bank account. I used to, but as I said, I've been putting my money up my nose. I paid all my bills off with our last lick. My mortgage on my condo was caught up. I even caught up on my car payment. Now, I was broke. I didn't know how I would play this off in Miami. I wasn't broke broke, but compared to what I should have, I was. I wouldn't be able to ball in Miami like I wanted to.

I heard Keena blowing her horn outside, so I grabbed my bags, set my alarm, and headed out the door.

"Bitch, are you ready to turn up in Miami?" She began to give me the rundown on the nigga name Peter whom they called Black.

"Look, Kim. This nigga don't trust too many people. We gotta get him to trust us. We're cousins from Atlanta. We came to Miami for something new. That's the role we are playing."

"OK," I replied. After that, I tuned her out. My mind drifted to my mom. Today was her birthday. She would have been 51. I missed my mom. That coward took her from me. I didn't talk much about my mom. Not even to Keena. It hurt too bad. I was close to my mom. I never understood why she wouldn't leave that no-good bastard. Bishop was his name. I say *was* because he was no longer living. I killed that nigga just like he killed my mom. Nobody knew I had anything to do with his death. I thought back to the day my mom was killed.

I had just walked in the door from school. I heard them in their room arguing, which was nothing new. This went on daily in my house. Bishop was asking my mom why our neighbor Tony was in our driveway.

"Bishop, gon' ahead with that mess. I already told you he was looking at my car. You know he's a mechanic. I been telling you for two weeks that something is going on with my car."

"So that give you a reason to be all up in that nigga's face?"

I couldn't understand what Bishop was tripping for. The whole Windsong Trails knew he was cheating on my mom. That's the name of the neighborhood we were staying in. Exit four is what all the young kids be screaming these days.

"Bishop, he was not in my face. All he was trying to do is figure out what was going on with my car."

"Bitch, are you trying to say I'm lying?"

I heard him smack my mom in her face. I wanted so badly to help her. I knew it wouldn't do any good, though. She wasn't going to leave him. Once she got tired of putting up with him, then she would. My mom surprised me this time, though. She did something she had never done before. She hit Bishop back. I guess she *was* tired. The smack to his face was so loud it echoed throughout the house. I was happy she had hit him back, but that hit caused her an early death.

"Bitch, did you just hit me?"

"Yes, I did. I'm tired of you putting your hands on me, nigga. That was your last time."

By this time, I had moved closer to her bedroom. I was looking at them through the crack in the door. My mom looked up and saw me standing there. I saw something different in her eyes this time. She was tired of Bishop. I was prepared to help her jump on him.

"What you gonna do if I hit you again? Oh, you think you're bad."

"Hit me again, and you'll see."

Of course, he hit her again. Next, I heard a bunch of thumping. Then I heard a gun go off. I flew into the room as Bishop ran out of the room right past me. My mom was on the floor in a puddle of blood. I dialed 911. I didn't have any family to call. My mom never talked about her family, and I didn't have a clue who my dad was. She never talked about him either. The police never found Bishop . . . but I did. I saw him coming out of a liquor house about four years ago. I asked him one question. I wanted to know why he killed my mom. His response was, "Fuck that bitch." I lost my mind. I shot him and never looked back.

The next day, I saw it all on the news. The police didn't have any suspects. That's all I needed to hear. Case closed in my eyes. I had no remorse.

"Earth to Kim."

"Huh?" I asked with a puzzled look.

"I have been calling your name. You didn't answer."

"My fault, Keena. I was thinking about my mom. Today would have been her birthday."

"Kim, you should have said something. We could have taken some flowers to her grave. I never knew. You don't discuss that part of your life with me."

"I know I don't. It's too painful to me." As I finished my sentence, we pulled into a parking spot at the airport. I grabbed my bags, and we walked through the terminal. Just that fast, I snapped back to reality.

Chapter 8

Keena

It was ninety-eight degrees in Miami as we walked out of the airport. It was only eighty-five degrees back in Charlotte. The weather here was totally different. We caught a shuttle to Enterprise rental car. I rented a Range Rover for a month. I hope I didn't need it longer than that. Then I drove us to our hotel.

Once we got to our room, I pulled out my iPad. I had been following Black's birthday party on Twitter. It was an all-white affair. He had hired Frute by Tha Pound entertainment to host his party. I was familiar with the company because they were from Charlotte. I was happy for him. He was making a name for himself. The fact that he was hosting a party in Florida told the story. His name was spreading. I Googled the closest mall. We had to be fly. I knew Kim did not really have any money. She did not know that I knew that. Everything was on me. When this was over, we were going to have a long talk. My white girl Becky told me Kim had emptied her bank account. I'll see if she'll tell me on her own first.

I decided we would hit Sunset Mall on Sunset Boulevard in South Miami.

"Get ready so that we can hit the mall, Kim. Our outfits gotta be on point tonight. We need to make sure we stand out." I saw the expression on her face, but I chose to ignore it.

"This one's on me," I winked at her.

We pulled up to the mall, and I swooped my car into a parking space.

"We're not going to be in here long, Kim."

I spent well over $3,000 at the mall. I bought myself a white sleeveless Hervé Léger dress and a pair of zebra print Red Bottoms. Kim picked out a white Kate Spade dress with one shoulder and a pair of black Red Bottoms. Then we headed back to our hotel room.

The party was jumping when we walked through the door. I must admit, the party planner did their thing. The place was decorated in silver, black, and white. Women were on swings hanging from the ceiling. Some were even in a cage dancing. There were even a few panthers pacing in cages. I knew I had to make my way into VIP even though plenty of women were already there with the same motive as I was . . . to catch his eye.

It was an open bar. I was over at the bar getting a Mango Peach Sangria when I spotted him. The DJ had just announced that he was in the building. Suddenly, women were flocking all around him. I knew to play it cool. Men usually went after the one that was playing hard to get. I turned around with my drink in my hand and locked eyes with him. Then I walked right past him and over to Kim. I knew he was watching me. I could feel his eyes on me. I mean, not to toot my own horn or anything, but I *am* a bad bitch. I knew that I was killing the whole scene tonight. There was not a bitch in sight that looked better than me.

I was about to strike up a conversation with Kim when some lame stepped in between us.

"Hey, sexy ladies," he greeted us.

"Hey," we both said at the same time. He grabbed Kim's hand. She gently snatched it away. She knew not to make a scene. Some lady walked by in some cheap-ass tights, and he quickly dismissed us. I wasn't mad at him. I turned around . . . and there was Peter again. He walked over toward me.

"Hi. I'm Black." He reached his hand out to me. I just looked at him. His pictures did him no justice. This man was *fine*. When he smiled, I saw he only had one dimple on his right cheek. He also had a scar right above his left eye. I knew I had to find out about that. I don't know how I missed that. He stood about six feet two. His skin tone was a Hershey dark chocolate, and the waves in his head were so deep, that I was getting seasick. He had a diamond so big in his ears that I was bedazzled. And that pinky ring was on point too. That nigga was iced out. I had to refocus. He was making my panties wet.

"I don't shake people's hands. I don't know where your hands have been."

He started laughing at me. "Oh, you don't know where my hands been at?"

"No, I don't even know you." I tried to walk around him. I had to play the role. He grabbed me by my arm. I turned around. I knew not to be nasty with him, but I had to be firm.

"I don't know you, and you don't know me. Don't be putting your hands on me." I attempted to walk off again. This time, he didn't stop me. I heard him yelling something, though.

"It's OK, li'l mama. I'll break you down." I heard his friends laughing. I was not going to give in tonight. I had to make him *want* me and *trust* me. I was going to show up everywhere he was at.

"Li'l mama feisty, ain't she?" I heard one of his friends say. I looked up, and it was his best friend, Seth. I knew it was his best friend because I had also done my homework on him. That nigga also had plenty of money, but he was not my target. I wanted the HNIC, which was Peter. *He* was the head nigga in charge. I watched the women flock around him for the rest of the night. He was turning all of them down.

Chapter 9

Black

I watched li'l mama the whole night. She was dismissing niggas left and right. To me, that meant she wasn't thirsty. The niggas that were trying to holla at her were all ballers too. Everyone in Miami knew they had money. I even watched T.I. walk by her. All the other women were doing everything they could to get his attention. She acted as if he didn't even matter. There were only one or two things that could be going on here. Either she's not from here, or a nigga with money doesn't impress her because she had her own. Either way, I was intrigued. She turned me down, and *nobody* turned down Black. She did not even tell me her name. I was not worried about it, though. Miami is my city. Nothing got past me. Women came up to me all night, wishing me a happy birthday. I know a few of them were secretly wanting me to take them home, but I was not into all of that. I didn't trust too many people. Nobody except my mom and sister even knew where I lay my head. I would typically go to other women's homes or take them to a cheap hotel.

They never cared where I took them as long as they could say they fucked me. I shook my head at the thought. It was a damn shame how some women acted at times. I enjoyed the rest of my night.

The following day, I went to my mom's house to take her to Publix on West Avenue. This was our ritual every Sunday. I never missed one Sunday with my mom. I was all she had other than my little sister. I would go to war behind those two. I pulled into my mom's driveway, and my little sister was on the porch talking to some li'l nigga. I was mad as hell. She's only 13. Immediately, I jumped out of the car.

"Who is this little nigga, Paulina?"

She started laughing. I didn't see shit funny. She was gonna make me catch a case.

"Calm down, Peter. This is Steven. His family just moved here from North Carolina. He was only introducing himself to me."

My sister didn't know me by Black. She didn't even know that side of me.

I looked at that li'l nigga as I stuck my hand out to shake his. I could tell I had scared him.

"I'm Peter. Welcome to Miami." Then I walked past them and into the house.

"Hey, Ma." I greeted her with a kiss. She was looking at me all crazy.

"What's up, Ma? Why are you looking at me like that?"

"Oh, you know why."

"No, I don't, Ma."

"You were ready to hurt that little boy. You *do* know one day she's going to have a boyfriend, don't you?"

"Whatever, Ma. I ain't trying to think about that right now. Are you ready to go to the store?"

"Yes. Let me grab my purse."

I walked out the door ahead of my mom. "Tell your little friend bye, Paulina, and come on."

"Do I have to go?"

I just looked at her. She already knew what that meant. She told Steven, or whatever his name was, that she had to go.

"Don't make me do something to your boyfriend," I jokingly said to her as I mushed her in the back of the head.

"That is *not* my boyfriend."

"Who is your boyfriend then?"

"I don't have one."

"You better not."

We were walking down the dry foods aisle when I spotted her. It was the lady from last night. The mystery lady that turned me down. She looked up at me at the same time I was looking at her. Then she looked away—the nerve of her. I can't believe she rolled her eyes at me. I didn't even care. As I said, Miami is my motherfucking city. I walked up to her with a big-ass grin on my face.

"Hey, Miss Lady."

"Hey," she said, all dry.

"Are you going to tell me your name today?"

"Why should I?"

"I told you mine."

"I didn't ask you for your name. You volunteered it."

I started laughing because she was right.

"Keena." Her homegirl from last night walked up and called her name. She blew her breath and rolled her eyes upward. I knew she was pissed off that I now knew her name.

"Oh, OK, so Keena it is. Well, Miss Keena, what is the rest of your name?"

"What are you talking about?"

"What goes behind Keena?"

"Nothing. It's just Keena." She walked off.

"Who was that?" my little sister asked me after I walked back over to her and my mom.

"That is my future wife. She just doesn't know it yet."

"She must be something special. I ain't never heard you say that about a woman before. Well, since . . ." She didn't finish her sentence. She saw the reaction on my face. "My fault, baby," my mom said.

"It's OK. She is, Mama. She's my future wife."

Chapter 10

Keena

I was really pissed at Kim, and I would let her have it once we got into the car. She told that nigga my name. He was not supposed to know my damn name. He was our lick, but now he knows my damn name. I just looked at her ass.

"What?"

"So, you *really* don't know what the fuck you just did?"

"If I knew, I wouldn't be asking."

I left the cart in the middle of the aisle and headed back to the truck. It was a decoy anyway. I knew Black was going to be in that store.

When Kim got into the car, I went in on her.

"You called my damn name out, Kim. You know that is a big no-no. He is *not* supposed to know my real name."

"My fault, Keena. Damn, I did fuck up."

"Yeah, you been fucking up a lot lately. Bone almost killed your ass. Did you forget about *that?* I went against my better judgment on that, so I guess that one is *my* fault."

I sped out of the parking lot and headed back toward the hotel. The whole drive, I was trying to figure out what was wrong with Kim.

Chapter 11

Kim

Keena didn't have to talk to me like that. Damn, I needed a hit bad. I had some with me. I just had to get away from her ass for a little while. Shit, the way I was feeling, fuck her. I don't know who she thinks she is talking to me all crazy anyway. She ain't my boss. We were equal partners in this shit. Yes, I know I shouldn't have said her name, but how was I supposed to know he was there when I bent the damn corner? She shouldn't have been cupcaking with his ass.

I went straight to my room when we returned to the hotel and searched my bags until I found what I was looking for. My mouth was watering because I was anticipating the taste of the coke.

I placed it on the nightstand that was beside the bed. Then I grabbed a card out of my purse and separated it into two lines.

I lay my head back on the pillow after sniffing the first line. That shit was so strong it had my nose running. I just wanted to enjoy my high. I reached over to sniff the second line and felt the rush go straight to my head.

I jumped when I heard the banging on my door. I looked at my phone. It was ten at night. I didn't mean to sleep that long. I knew it was Keena at the door because I had over ten missed calls from her ass. What the fuck does this bitch want, I asked myself. I was still feeling salty from earlier. I looked at the nightstand. It still had powder residue on it.

"Wait a minute, Keena. Damn."

I rushed to clean up my mess before I let her in.

"What's up?" I asked her as I opened the door.

"Shit, you tell me. I been calling you for a while."

"I fell asleep." I know this bitch didn't come to my room to check me about why I didn't answer my damn phone. Shit, last I checked, *I* paid the phone bill.

"Is that all you wanted? If so, I'm going back to sleep."

"I was worried about you, Kim, that's all. You been off lately. What's going on with you?"

I chitchatted with Keena for a little bit before seeing her out of my room. I wanted to finish enjoying the rest of my high.

Black

I couldn't get shorty off my mind. I had been thinking about her since the night of my party. I didn't trust too many people. I stopped trusting people the day I saw my dad's best friend kill him. That was also the day my heart turned cold. At the time, I couldn't figure out why he would want to kill my dad. My dad didn't sell any drugs. He was a detective for Miami PD. He was a hardworking man that went to work every day.

I thought back to the day of my father's murder. It was March, and it had been raining for three days. I was home on spring break. My mom was with her sister playing bingo. I heard my dad pull into the driveway. I was waiting on him to enter the door. I had straight As on my report card, and he had promised to take me to the Miami Heat game. He was taking longer than usual, so I looked out the window to see what was taking him so long. I saw him outside talking to Bookie with the rain beating down their faces. My dad's whole demeanor had changed, so I knew they were arguing. I went to the front door to see if I could hear them. This was Uncle Bookie. What in the world could they possibly have fallen out about? Uncle Bookie was my godfather. Ever since my eyes opened, he has been in the picture. I have never seen them even raise their voice to each other before. I heard my father say, "Bookie, I just cannot do it."

"Come on, Paul. This is me. I need you to do this for me."

"Bookie, Sharon is pregnant. I cannot lose my job behind your mess. I've told you to stop fucking with those Italians."

"If you don't get those drugs back, I'm a dead man. I don't have the money to repay those crazy-ass wops."

"Bookie, I love you, man, but I can't do it. I have already put my career on the line by destroying evidence from that murder you did. I can't do this anymore. All my life, I've wanted to be a cop. You, of all people, know that."

"Oh, so it's like that, Paul? Your saying, fuck me?"

"Bookie, I ain't said nothing. That was all you're saying."

"Since you won't help me, that means you don't care about my life. Since you don't care about mine, then I don't care about your life either."

"Bookie, what are you talking about?" My dad realized Bookie had a gun in his hand.

"Bookie, what are you doing, man?"

That's when I heard the gunshot, and my dad fell on his back. Bookie looked up and saw me and fired at me.

I took off running, and he was right behind me. I could not believe Bookie had just shot my dad and was now gunning for me.

Little did Bookie know my dad's partner was on the way to the house, and he heard the gunshots. While Bookie was chasing me, Dad's partner was chasing him. All I heard was *Pop! Pop! Pow! Argh!* Bookie yelled out in pain. He was hit by one of the bullets. I stopped dead in my tracks when I heard my father's partner call out my name.

"Peter!"

I ran full speed toward him. He was already speaking on his radio.

"Officer down. Officer down." He gave them all the info they needed. Then he waited on the medics to come and get Bookie. When we got back to my house, cops were everywhere. My mom was standing in the driveway screaming. My aunt was trying to calm her down and keep her from falling. She kept telling Mom to be careful because she was pregnant.

On March 11, 2001, my sister came into this world, and my dad took his last breath. People say when somebody is born, somebody dies typically. I just hate it was my dad.

They gave Bookie life in prison, but his time was cut short. I used my inside connections a few years ago and had him killed.

I drove down Palmetto Expressway, bumping my Fetty Wap "Trap Queen." I was headed home with shorty heavy on my mind. I was really feeling the lyrics today for some reason. I wanted her to be *my* trap queen but in a positive way.

I'm like, "Hey, what's up? Hello. Seen yo' pretty ass soon as you came in that door. I just wanna chill, got a sack for us to roll. Married to the money, introduced her to my stove. Showed her how to whip it, now she remixin' for low She my trap queen."

I pulled into the garage of my minimansion. I loved this house. I picked it out, thinking about settling down and having some kids one day. My mom put her touch on it, of course. It has six bedrooms and seven bathrooms. I also have a three-bedroom, two-bath pool house in the back. This house is too big for just me. And I'm getting tired of this life. I want to settle down soon, and Ms. Keena seems to be the one. She just does not know it yet.

Kim

I rolled over and looked at the time on my phone. It was seven in the morning, and I had a text message from Ashton. I had forgotten all about him. I laughed when I read his message.

Ashton: U miss me?
Me: I don't even know u.
Ashton: So that's what I'm tryin'a do.
Me: U r silly. U don't know me either.
Ashton: So, what's up?
Me: Go to sleep.
Ashton: Come sleep with me.
Me: Out of town.
Ashton: So, if u wasn't, would u come lie with me?
Me: I didn't say all that.
Ashton: I will wear u down, woman.
Me: lol

I heard my stomach growling. I was so high yesterday that I didn't even eat, so I decided to get dressed and head downstairs to grab a bite. I was debating if I should ask Keena to join me. I decided not to. She was starting to get on my damn nerves. I knew it was just my conscience because I was trying to hide the fact that I was getting high. I was also going to hit the beach. I had peeped that view from my hotel room. Shit, we're in Miami, so I may as well enjoy myself.

After eating breakfast, I returned to my room and put on my all-black, two-piece Michael Kors bathing suit and my all-black thong Michael Kors sandals. I looked in the full-length mirror and saw I was killing it. It hugged all my curves just right. As a finishing touch, I put on my Aviator Ray-Ban shades and walked out the door.

I was lying on the beach with my eyes closed when I felt somebody standing over me. I removed my shades and was struck by the sight before me. He reminded me of the rapper Future. He looked so much like him that I had to look again. I'm crazy about Future, so you know my head was gone.

"Yes?" I tried to say with an attitude, but I was so caught up with how he looks it didn't even come out like that. He started laughing at me.

"What's so funny?" This time, I had an attitude.

"You know you're too cute to have that attitude. My name is Seth." He stuck his hand out for me to shake it. I just looked at his hand. I do not shake people's hands. He took the hint and withdrew it.

"I'm Shonte." I gave him my fake name that we used when we were on our licks.

"Nice to meet you, Shonte. Where are you from?"

"Atlanta." I didn't know him. There was no way I was telling him where I was really from.

"How long are you here for?"

"I relocated here along with my cousin."

"Well, Shonte, put your number in my phone." He pushed his phone toward me. I hesitated at first.

"What's the problem?"

I noticed his dimples for the first time. They were so deep.

"Nothing," I said as I grabbed his phone. I put my number in it and gave it back to him. I had two phones. One was for Shonte, and the other one was for Kim. I didn't like getting confused, so that's why I had two.

"I'm gonna give you a call, Shonte." I vaguely glanced back at him before he walked off. He looked a little too familiar to me, but I couldn't place it. I ain't from around here, so I really couldn't figure out where I would know him from, so I just shook it off. He glanced back at me before he walked off. I got up after he left.

I ran into Keena on the way back to my room.

"Where you been?"

"Minding my own business."

"Well, my fault," she said as she walked off. I did not have time to entertain her, so I let her leave.

Chapter 12

Keena

I don't know what is getting into Kim. After this lick, I think we need to go our separate ways. It will hurt me because we've been friends so long, but I can't let anybody hinder me. I'm all I got. I have family, but they got ghost after my dad got killed. They did not even take me in, forcing me into foster care and group homes.

Today is Monday, and I had to be wherever Peter was. He worked out at Planet Fitness on Eighth Street every Monday, Wednesday, and Friday, so I grabbed my workout clothes and headed to the parking garage. I wanted to get there before him. I decided to leave Kim behind. I did not have time for her fuckups today. Since Black already knew my real name, I had to keep it that way. *Damn, Kim,* I thought to myself.

I was on the treadmill when Black finally walked into the gym. He hadn't noticed me yet. I looked away and switched the music on my iPod to Yo Gotti and Nicki Minaj, "Down in the DM."

I seen your girl post her BM, so I hit her in her DM, All eyes, yeah, I see 'em, yeah, that's your man? I hate to be him (whoop). It goes down in the DM.

I was running on the treadmill and rapping the lyrics to the song when I felt a tap on my shoulder. I pulled off my headset.

"What?" I said with an attitude. "If I didn't know any better, I would think you're following me. Like, what the hell? First the grocery store, and now here?"

"Hold on, li'l mama, I ain't following you. I work out here three days a week. Maybe *you* are following *me*. I ain't never saw you here before."

I hopped off the treadmill. I was now in his face. "Hi, let me formally introduce myself because it doesn't seem like you're going anywhere. I'm Keena." He grabbed me in a warm embrace. I was embarrassed. I was sweaty, so I pulled back fast. He caught on because he started laughing.

"Don't be laughing at me."

"My fault, but you *are* funny. I guess you didn't want me to smell your funky butt," he said as he burst out laughing again. I admit I had to laugh too.

I was about to walk out the door when I heard Black call my name. I turned around to face him.

"Let me get your number, Keena. I'd love to take you out."

I gave him my number and walked off.

Chapter 13

Black

I stood in the parking lot and watched Keena get into her car. I don't know what it is about this girl. It's been a long time since I've shown interest in a woman. Women come a dime a dozen to me. I just stick'em and move because I don't trust any of those gold-digging hoes. I knew if I got with Keena, I would have to protect her. I did not want anything to happen to her because a jealous-ass nigga wanted to take her out to get at me. I thought back to the only girlfriend I ever had.

Ebony was her name. She was everything I wanted in a woman. She genuinely loved me. She always put my needs before hers, and that got her killed. She was a student at Florida A&M University. I was supposed to come to the football game that day and watch her from the stands. It was the Florida Blue Classic game and one of the season's biggest games. The game was in Orlando, and fans came from around the world. This was huge. My baby was the head cheerleader, so you know I had to be in attendance. She had been talking about this game all week. I still remember our conversation.

"Peter, promise me you'll be there. We're playing Bethune-Cookman. You know they're our biggest rival." She always called me Peter.

"Baby, I wouldn't miss your game for nothing in this world," I said as I wrapped my arms around her and planted a kiss on her lips. They tasted so sweet. She always wore that cotton candy lip gloss. She playfully pushed me off her. We were standing in front of Truth Hall, the female dorm she stayed in. I was dropping her back off at school after a long night of passion. She had to be back at the school to travel with the team. They had a three-hour forty-minute ride. It was six in the morning. The game started at one, so that gave me a few hours to handle my business before making that trip.

I looked up at the sky. It was a gloomy day for it to be November. Something just didn't feel right. I had a funny feeling that I couldn't shake. I kissed Ebony again as I told her I'd see her later. If I knew that was the last time I would see her alive, I never would have left her.

I got caught up in some street business and lost track of time, but I was outside Orlando. I called Ebony because I knew the game was over. It was all over 103.1, the popular radio station in Orlando. Bethune-Cookman had beaten Florida. The score was twenty-one to sixteen. I didn't want her to be mad at me and knew I had some making up to do.

"Hello," she answered on the first ring. She had a smile in her voice when she should have been cussing me out, but she didn't. Ebony rarely got mad at me. She understood my life, and she accepted me for who I was.

"Baby, where are you? Please don't be mad at me."

"Peter, you know I'm not mad at you. I am a little disappointed because I did want you to see me cheer in my first big game. You know I do not have anybody here but you. My family's in Georgia."

"Baby, I know. But listen, I'm about to scoop you and take you back to my crib. Where are you?"

"I'm about to walk through the courtyard at the hotel. We're staying at the Embassy Suites downtown. I'm not even sure if I can leave. I thought you were going to stay the night. You know the city is alive right now." The next thing I heard was a gunshot.

"Ebony, what's going on?" I said with panic in my voice. My worst fear was coming to pass right before my eyes—someone killing somebody I loved.

"Bitch, if you don't tell me where the fuck Black lay his head, I will blow your fucking brains out."

"I don't know where his house is. Even if I did, I wouldn't tell you," she said calmly.

I yelled through the phone, "I'm on my way. Please, don't kill her." I'd never begged for anything, but I was begging for Ebony's life. Finally, somebody named Turk picked up the phone.

"Too late, Black. I'm going to kill this bitch. I've been watching her for a while. I could never catch you slipping, and I been waiting on this moment. You are too cocky for me. You think you a kingpin, nigga? Before I kill her, I want to taste this pussy while you listen to her scream."

"Nigga, you can have it all. Just don't kill her."

"Nah, nigga, I don't want your money. This shit right here is personal."

I later discovered that Turk was my godfather Bookie's son, whom we never knew anything about. Bookie had a secret affair with Turk's mom, and Turk was a secret. Bookie was married at the time, and his wife couldn't have any kids.

All I saw was red. I was running all the red lights and stop signs. I was forty-five minutes from downtown. I swear I got there in ten minutes. Time was at a standstill as I drove my Cadillac Escalade in the hotel's parking lot. By this time, the police, an ambulance, and firetrucks were everywhere. I hopped out of the truck and ran toward them. My heart stopped when I saw her lying on the ground, still in her cheerleading uniform. Those orange and green colors are what stood out.

The orange was stained with blood. Nobody had even bothered to cover her up. My entire world was over. I ran to her body, and a police officer grabbed me. Today was not the day. I was going to jail if he did not let me go.

"Sir, you have to step away from the scene."

Then I heard somebody in the background saying that I was her boyfriend. I kneeled right by her body.

"Ebony, please, don't leave me. Please, baby, wake up." I knew she was dead, but I needed her. She was my better half. There is no way God was punishing me like this. I lifted her head and kissed her forehead. She had a bullet by her temple. I would tear up Florida until I got to the bottom of this.

I slowly walked back to my truck. I heard the officers calling out to me, but I don't talk to pigs. I had nothing to say. I made a phone call to my man, Seth. I told him to put out a hundred-thousand-dollar reward for any information about who had killed Ebony. In less than twenty-four hours, somebody gave up Turk.

I snapped back to the present when I heard Keena blowing her horn at me as she sped off. After that, I hopped in my old-school Chevy, headed home to shower, and called my man Seth on the way to the crib.

"Yo, Seth," I said as soon as he picked up the phone, "do you remember shorty from my birthday party? The light-skinned chick that had a damn attitude all night."

"Yeah, the one that shut you down," he said, laughing.

"Man, shut the hell up. That shit ain't funny."

"Yes, it is. You couldn't believe she turned you down. *Nobody* turns you down." He was still laughing.

"You're right. Nobody," I said as I joined in on his laughter.

"Well, ole girl did. She showed you no mercy."

"Shut up, man. Well, anyway, I finally broke shorty down."

"I'm happy for you. I ain't seen you go this hard for a female since Ebony." He got quiet. I know he hated letting Ebony's name slip out of his mouth. "My fault, man."

"You're okay. I was thinking about her earlier today. It's gotten a little easier. Maybe Keena can help ease my mind. I like her, man, and I don't even know her."

"Just be careful, man." We chatted for a bit longer, and then I hung up.

After my shower, I shot Keena a text.

Black: What's up, shorty?

I flopped down on my bed and turned on my seventy-inch smart TV while waiting for her to respond. I landed on *Stevie J*'s bitch-ass show. I didn't care for him, but Joseline was bad as hell. The "Puerto Rican Princess" is what she called herself. I wish they would get her some speech lessons, though. I don't see how Stevie puts up with the way she talks. I couldn't deal with that shit.

I must have dozed off because I woke up to the sound of my phone ringing. It was my mom. I missed her call. I saw that she had called me over ten times. I knew something was wrong. I was almost scared to call her back. She *never* called me back-to-back like that.

"What's up, Ma?"

She was hysterical when she answered the phone. "Oh my God, Peter. She's gone."

I immediately jumped up and grabbed my keys. "Who's gone, Ma? What are you talking about?"

"Your sister. Paulina is gone."

I went into panic mode. "Ma, what do you mean she's gone?"

"She never came home from school."

I looked at the time on my cell phone. It was almost nine p.m. I must have been exhausted. I can't believe I slept that long.

"Ma, why are you just now calling me?" I was in my car by now and rubbed my hands over my head, which I did when my mind was all over the place.

I got to my mom's house in record time. I didn't even have the car in park, and my mom ran out the door.

"Peter, I don't know where she's at. I've been calling her phone, and none of her friends have heard from her."

I got on the phone with my crew. I explained what was going on. After I hung up, I began to pray. That was something I had not done in a long time. I did not think God answered my prayers, but this was my baby sister. I could not lose her. My mind immediately went back to Ebony. Lord, this could not be happening again.

Hours had passed, and still no word on Paulina. I had my street soldiers combing the streets looking for her. I didn't want to leave my mom, but I was about to go crazy. I felt like I needed to be out there with them.

Keena had texted my phone, but I didn't want to talk to nobody. I wanted my sister. It was three in the morning when I got the phone call. It was from one of my street soldiers named Kenwa.

"Black, we found her behind Booker T. Washington High School."

I held my breath. "Is she OK?"

He got quiet. "Man, she's been raped. What do you want me to do?" I could hear the sadness in his voice.

"Take her to Holtz Children's Hospital. I'll meet you there." I turned around, and my mom had her hand over her mouth. Tears were streaming down her face. She heard the conversation. There was no need to repeat it.

"Oh God!" She let off a loud, painful scream. "God, no. Not my baby."

My mom hopped out of the car before I could even park. That was her baby. I parked in front of the hospital.

"Sir, you cannot park your car here. If you leave it, we will tow it." I turned around and looked at him. "Oh, man, hey, Black. I didn't know that was you. Throw me your keys. I'll move it for you." I tossed him my keys, then ran to the receptionist's desk. Immediately, I spotted Kenwa.

"I checked her in, but they won't tell me anything. They say I ain't no kin to her."

I walked up to the receptionist's desk and instantly regretted going there. Sitting behind the desk was this dizzy-ass broad name Zeena who I had slept with once. She never got over how I just hit it and never talked to her ass again. Tonight was not the night, though. I would cuss her ass out if she made it hard for me.

"I need to find out about my little sister. She was just brought in here. Paulina Jones."

She rolled her eyes, but to my surprise, she gave me the information without an attitude. I guess she acted a different way at work.

"Hold on, Black. Let me call back there to the nurse. Somebody needs to escort you back."

A few minutes later, a nurse came and got us. The doctor was in the room when we walked in. My sister looked terrible. She had been beaten. Bruises covered her body. Her lip was busted, and her eye was swollen shut. Her legs were bloody. I could not even look at that. My mom looked over at me. Immediately, I knocked all the stuff off the table as I walked out of the room. I was mad as hell. Somebody was going to pay for this shit.

I looked at my phone because I had just got a text message from Keena. I wondered what she was doing up.

Keena: I got up to go to the bathroom. I know ur prob asleep.

Me: Ur just nasty. That's tmi (too much information), but for real, I'm mad as hell.

Keena: Sorry to hear that. May I ask u what's wrong?

I wasn't sure if I wanted to tell her. I didn't really know her, but I felt comfortable around her for some reason.

Me: Somebody just raped my fucking sister. I'm at the hospital.

I thought she would text me back, but she called instead.

"Hello." She sounded out of breath. "I'm putting my clothes on. What hospital are you at?"

I was a little taken aback. I didn't even know this damn girl, but she was ready to run to the hospital to be by my side.

"Li'l mama, you don't have to come up here. I'm good."

"I know I don't have to come, but I am. I didn't ask you if you were good because I know you're not. Now, what hospital are you at? I'm already walking to my car."

Li'l mama was feisty. I liked that. She has already scored brownie points with me.

"I'm at Holtz."

She hung up the phone.

Chapter 14

Keena

My heart went out to Black's sister. I really did feel bad for her. I also knew this was the perfect opportunity to win him over. I punched the hospital into my GPS and headed out that way, then called Black once I arrived. I wanted him to meet me out front.

"Hello," he answered on the first ring.

"Can you meet me at the door?"

"Yes, here I come."

I followed him to the waiting room. "Thank you for coming, li'l mama. That means a lot to a nigga." I could see the pain all over his face. I listened to him while he talked. When he was done, I got up out of my seat and hugged him. He hugged me tight and placed his head on my shoulder. He was sitting down, and I was standing up. Hell, I was only five foot four. He was six foot two. I just let him rest there.

I watched as his mom came out. He ran over and talked to her. She looked over at me and gave me a weak smile. I dismissed it. I knew what she was going through because she was upset about her daughter.

It was almost ten in the morning when I returned to the hotel. I was exhausted. I hopped in the shower and lay across the bed, naked.

I woke up around five to Kim beating on my door and a text message from Joc. I read his text while walking to the door to let Kim in.

Joc: What's up? I haven't heard from u.

Me: U know how it goes.

"Damn, Keena. Put on some damn clothes. I don't want to see your naked ass." I had forgotten I didn't have on any clothes, so I quickly walked over to the dresser and grabbed a T-shirt and some panties. Then my text alert went off again. I thought it was from Joc, but it was Black.

Black: I can't thank u enough for last night.

Me: It was nothing.

Black: Let me take u out. It's the least I can do.

Me: U don't owe me anything. It was from the heart.

The next thing I knew, my phone was ringing. It was Black. I looked over to see what Kim was doing before I answered. She was resting on my bed and had my iPad in her hand. I assumed she was reading a book.

"Hello."

"What's up, li'l mama? I'm not big on texting. I'd rather talk on the phone."

"How is your sister doing?"

"She is doing as OK as she can be. She's pretty shaken up, though. I got my ear to the streets. She said there were two of them. I got a name on one of them. His dumb friend said his name. Both of them are lying low, I'm sure."

"Well, I got her in my prayers."

We talked a little while longer. He asked me to dinner, but I declined. I did not want to make it easy for him. I wanted *him* to chase *me*. I had to have a tight grip on Peter Jones. He was not easy to take down. At 27, he was already worth over $50 million. He had businesses all over the world. This was not just a robbery. I could not just rob him. It ain't like he had millions of dollars lying around. I had to get his bank account information. I was going to be in Miami for a while, but it would be well worth it. I had plans to find a nice little condominium for Kim and me. I had prepaid my mortgage back home for a few months.

I threw a pillow at Kim. "Bitch, what are you doing with my iPad?" She didn't respond. She just rolled her eyes at me.

"You don't hear me talking to you, Kim?"

"I'm reading a damn book called *What Hurts the Most?* by some author name Tynessa. It seems to be a surprisingly enjoyable book." Kim has always liked to read. We both do, but she reads more than I do. I made a mental note to read that book once she finished. I had been hearing about that book all over Facebook. I overlooked Kim's attitude, but I hope she doesn't think it went unnoticed.

My stomach started growling. I was hungry. Kim looked up at me. "So, where are we eating at?"

"Well, let's hit Dolphin Mall first. We can eat there. I also gotta find us a condo. We're going to be here awhile. We can't keep living in this hotel." I caught Kim up on what was happening, and then she returned to her room to get dressed.

Chapter 15

Kim

Keena was really starting to get on my damn nerves. She is sitting on her high horse like her shit don't stink. Who decided *she* was the one that was supposed to snatch Black? I mean, like, *really,* Keena? Did she forget she was a virgin? A nigga like Black is going to want some pussy. He is the man in Miami. I did my research too.

I put on my clothes and met Keena in the lobby. I knew she could tell I had an attitude with her. At this point, I didn't care. After we left Miami, I was done with her ass. I looked over at her out of the side of my eye. I did not have a reason to dislike her. She was all I had. These drugs were really changing me. But I had to admit she was cute. She had on a cute little pink polo dress. It complimented her skin and went well with a pair of pink thong polo sandals.

I looked at my phone and saw a text message from Seth. I had forgotten about him. His text brought a smile to my face.

Seth: What's up, ma?

Me: Not much. At the mall with my cousin. U know how that goes.

Seth: Which one? Maybe I can come and fuck up some commas on u.

Now, *that* put an even bigger smile on my face. So I texted him back where I was, and he said he would call once he got there. However, I did not want Keena all in my business.

"Keena, I'll meet you in the food court once we're done. That way, we can get out quickly." She gave me a strange look, but I didn't care. She automatically snagged Black. We usually talk about who will play the role. As I said, I don't know how she will pull this off. A man of his caliber is going to want some ass.

I sat at a table in the middle of the food court, waiting on Seth. He had just called and said he was in the mall. Meanwhile, I was texting back and forth with Ashton. He had been texting me on a daily, trying to get to know me. I promised him a date once I got back to Charlotte. I looked up when I heard my name being called. Seth was sexy as hell. I looked over at him as he licked those LL Cool J lips. My pussy instantly became wet. I wanted to do him right then and there.

"What's up, ma?" he said as I looked into his beautiful gray eyes. I had the brightest smile on my face. I got up out of my seat, and he grabbed me and hugged me. I hugged him back.

"So, what store do you want to hit first, ma?"

"Well. Let's hit Polo first."

"I was hoping you would say that. I love Polo."

I looked at the time. It was a little after nine. The mall closed at nine thirty. I was really enjoying Seth. When I say he fucked up some commas on me, that's precisely what he did. He didn't hold anything back. I know he spent close to five thousand. We hit just about every store. I had so many bags surrounding me. He offered to take them to his car, but I wasn't ready for him to know where we were staying.

"It's OK, Seth. I came with my cousin, remember?"

“Yes, I know. I just didn’t want you to carry all those bags by yourself.”

“Just help me take them to our car.” I had the other set of keys. I wasn’t ready for Keena to see him yet.

After Seth loaded the car, I called Keena and told her I’d pick her up in front of the mall.

When Keena got in the car, she looked at me. “Damn, bitch, you’re cheesing,” she said with a smile.

“I’m good. Let’s just get something to eat. I’m still hungry.”

I headed to Joe’s Stone Crab on Washington Avenue.

Black

This shit that happened to my sister was fucking with a nigga. I had just got a call from Seth that they had those li’l niggas. I knew it was taking everything Seth had not to do them himself. Paulina was like a sister to him too. I knew he would let me handle it out of respect for me. So I hopped in my whip, heading to Little Haiti over on the north side of Miami. It was one of the toughest hoods in Miami. I had an empty apartment over there, which I used for moments like this.

I burst through the door and saw Seth had two li’l niggas tied to a chair. I kicked both chairs over one, behind the other. Then I snatched the tape off one of their mouths, whipped my gun out, and pointed it at one of the men’s heads.

“Start talking, motherfucker. Why did you rape my sister?”

“Man, fuck you,” he uttered with so much venom. I had to look a little closer to see if I knew him. He looked vaguely familiar, but I couldn’t place my finger on it.

"Wrong answer," I said as I shot him in his right knee. He screamed out in pain. "Nigga, shut the fuck up. Did you care when my sister was screaming and hollering for *you* to stop?

"Now, let's try this again." I snatched the tape off the other nigga's mouth this time.

"Why the fuck did you rape my sister?" I put a little more emphasis in it this time. He turned and looked at his partner. "I don't know what you're looking at him for. He can't help you." He didn't utter a word as he looked back at me, so I shot him in his right knee as well.

"One of y'all better start talking because my next shot will be to your most prized possession." The younger one of the two looked down at his dick with a look of shock on his face.

"Yes, motherfucker. I will shoot you in your dick."

The first nigga started talking. "You may as well kill us. I don't regret raping that bitch. You killed my pops. I couldn't wait to avenge his murder. I knew I couldn't get to you, so I snatched your sister. I was 9 years old when you and your crew ran up in my house. My dad put me in the closet. He already knew you was looking for him. I overheard him telling my mom that he had killed your girlfriend, and it was only a matter of time before you put it together."

I couldn't believe what I was hearing. This was Turk's son in front of me. I didn't know who the other nigga was, and I didn't care. Both of them violated my sister. Death was their only option. I killed Turk, and my sister got caught up in the crossfire. I didn't want to hear anymore.

Pow! Pow! I gave both of them a shot to the head. Blood oozed out of holes in the middle of their foreheads.

Walking out the door, I heard a few more gunshots. I knew it was Seth. Both of those niggas were already dead, but I knew Seth wanted to put a few bullets in them too.

Keena

I noticed that glow Kim had on her face. It came out of nowhere. I was not sure where it came from, but I was happy it was there. I was starting to feel like we were growing apart. She was all I had, so it saddened me.

As we returned to the hotel, a text came through from Joc. I let him know I would be in Miami for a while and would be looking for a place to stay.

I noticed all the bags Kim got out of the car. *That* had my mind racing. I knew she was broke, so I wondered where all these bags came from. I needed to keep my eye on her. I don't have time for whatever sneaky shit she was on. We were in a foreign city trying to take down one of the biggest kingpins in Miami. There was no time for sneaky shit.

While I was in the shower, my mind drifted off to Joc. We were not a couple, but I knew he liked me. I liked him too. If I were in a different lifestyle, he would be my man. I wondered what he thought of me. Only Kim knew that I was a virgin. I was a big flirt and a big tease, but I had never been in a relationship before. Therefore, no man had earned the right to my most prized possession. My daddy set the bar high. I knew my worth. A nigga had to come correct when he came at me or do not come at all.

I grabbed my iPad before plopping on the bed naked and researching a few vacant properties. Finally, I saw one that I liked. It was located on First Avenue and was called 4 Midtown Condo. It reminded me of my place back home.

Chapter 16

Kim

The following day, I woke up a little agitated. I knew I needed a hit. I poured a line on the nightstand. After the powder hit my nose, I started to relax. I also noticed that my supply was getting low. I was going to have to call back home to see if my supplier had any connects in Miami, so I immediately shot him a text message. He responded about ten minutes later. He said he would shoot his contact a text message asking him if I could get in touch with him. I turned on the television while I was waiting on his response. My whole mouth fell open as I listened to the news reporter.

> *"There was a shootout at Club Pulse in Orlando, Florida. Pulse is known as a gay club. Over fifty people were shot. The exact number of bodies is unclear. We will keep you updated as more facts come in. I am Jacey Birch reporting live from local 10 news."*

I immediately sent up prayers for the families. I am not gay, but all lives mattered. Then I heard my text alert go off, so I grabbed my phone. I was not ready for the message on my phone. He sent me Seth's information. I cannot ask Seth for that. There had to be another way.

Keena

When I woke up, I called the realtor about the condo I saw online. We set up an appointment for three. I got my hygiene together and sent Black a quick text message letting him know I was thinking about him. I did not want to seem too overbearing, but at the same time, I did not want him to lose interest. I needed this lick. I was done after this.

Me: Good morning; just checking on you and your sister.

Peter: She's good, and I would be even better if you let me take you out.

Me: lol

Peter: I am dead ass. Quit playing, ma.

Me: Let me think about it. I have a few errands to run first.

Peter: That's fair unless you want me to take you, lol

Me: I promise to call you later. Lol, I hope you can afford to feed me because I got a fat-girl appetite.

Peter: Don't worry about my pockets, ma. Like T.I. says, you can have whatever you like.

I tossed my phone on the bed after reading his last message. I had to admit he had just put a huge smile on my face. No man since my dad had ever put a smile on my face that bright. He was incredibly confident, like me. He saw something he liked, and he went after it. I reached for my suitcase to get something to wear.

Black

Li'l mama had my head gone. I looked at my phone. I had her saved as "Wifey." She just did not know it yet, but that is what she was going to be. I decided to go to my mom's house to check on her and my sis.

When I pulled up, Steven was in his driveway shooting basketball with an older-looking version of him. The boy looked up and ran over to where I was once he noticed it was me.

"I heard what happened to Paulina. How's she doing?" I noticed a hint of sadness in his voice.

"She's doing OK. I'll tell her you asked about her." Then just as I was about to walk into the house, the older version of him spoke.

"What's up, man? I'm Quan, Steven's older brother." He reached his hand out for a shake.

"My name is Peter," I told him as I reached my fist out for a pound. "Welcome to Miami," I yelled over my shoulder as I walked up the steps leading to my mom's front door.

"Ma," I yelled as I walked into the kitchen. It smelled good. I tried to look in one of the pots, but before I could get the lid off, my mom smacked my hand with a dish towel.

"Ouch, Ma, that hurt."

"It was supposed to hurt. You know better. I don't know where your hands been," she said with a smile.

"What are you cooking, Ma?"

"I'm cooking for the people who live here, so don't worry about it," she said as she threw the towel at me.

"Ma, don't play."

"Well, if you must know, I'm cooking all of your sister's favorites. I got barbeque ribs, macaroni and cheese, candied yams, broccoli and cheese casserole, and homemade biscuits. Oh, and before I forget, my famous sweet tea."

"Dang, Ma, you're not playing. Today ain't Sunday. You normally only cook like that on Sundays or holidays."

"Yes, I know, but I was trying to cheer up your sister."

I kissed my mom on the cheek. "You're the best, Ma." Then I walked off to check on my baby sister. She was sitting up in bed watching *White House Down* with Jamie Foxx. She smiled when she saw me. I sat on the bed beside her, and she wrapped her arms around my neck. I hugged my sister as she cried in my chest. That shit hurt me to my soul.

"Why did those men do that to me, Peter? I don't bother nobody."

I did not know how to answer her question, so I answered the best way I knew how. "Some people are just evil, Paulina. I promise you that will never happen again. When you get to feeling better, maybe I'll take you and your new boyfriend to Disney World." Her eyes lit up.

"Peter, I told you he is *not* my boyfriend."

I started laughing, and she joined in. I was happy to see that smile.

"Well, whatever he is, I will take y'all to Disney World."

"Can Erica come?" Erica was her best friend.

"Um, let me think about it."

She rolled her eyes and blew air out of her mouth. Then she threw her teddy bear at me. She knew I was just messing with her. She could have whatever she wanted. "Peter!"

I started laughing again. "Of course, Erica can come." It felt good to hear her laugh. My sister was my heart, and I would turn into Hurricane Katrina behind that one.

Chapter 17

Black

The Cleveland Cavaliers were playing the Golden State Warriors. I knew it was going down at the Yard House, a local sports bar off Lenox Avenue. Ms. Keena did not know it yet, but she would be my date for tonight. So I picked up the phone to call her.

"Hey, Peter." She answered on the third ring. She kind of caught me off guard with the "Peter." Only a few people called me that, and Ebony was one of them.

"Peter, huh?" I asked her.

"Yes, Peter. I do not do nicknames. I ain't one of your homeboys," she said with a chuckle.

"Oh." I let that roll off my tongue. Ebony had told me the same thing I remembered.

"Well, anyway, Ms. Keena, I ain't taking no for an answer. Tonight, you are going with me to watch the big game. So, when we get off the phone, text me your address. Be ready at six."

"Wow, you're very demanding, I see. From the sound of it, I don't have a choice."

"No, you really don't."

"Well, Mr. Peter, I will just meet you there."

"No, you will *not* meet me there, Keena. Stop being stubborn. What do I look like making you drive?"

"Well, I am staying in a hotel right now. I met my realtor yesterday to look at a condo."

"I don't care where you stay. Text me your address when we get off this phone, and I'll see you at six." I ended the call. A few minutes later, a text came through. I smiled when I saw it was from Keena.

Keena

I was going through my things, looking for my LeBron James jersey dress. It was a halter-style jersey dress. I put on my black Red Bottom heels and did a once-over in the mirror. Next, I put on black accessories and my clear Mac lip gloss. Once I was satisfied with my look, I sent Kim a text message letting her know what was up. A few minutes later, I heard a knock at the door. I assumed it was Kim, so I opened it up without looking. To my surprise, it was Peter with a big bouquet of yellow roses—my favorite color. I wonder if he knew that was my color. In his other hand, he held an edible arrangement. I love fruit. I stepped back, wearing a big Kool-Aid smile so he could come in.

"Thanks for the arrangements, both of them, and welcome to my temporary home. I'm ready if you are."

He grabbed my hand, and we walked out the door.

The bar was packed to capacity. Everybody there kept stopping Peter to say what's up. Finally, we were headed to the back of the bar when a chick stopped right in front of Peter. She placed her hand on his chest. I could tell he was a little uncomfortable with me standing beside him.

"What do you want, Zeena?" he stated as he gritted his teeth like he was agitated. I laughed at how similar our names were. I don't think Peter found any humor in this situation. I decided to see how things were going to play out. After all, he was not my man. I had no claims on him, so I was not about to cause a scene.

"How have you been, Black? When you're done entertaining *that* . . ." she waved her hand at me like I was not even standing there. This bitch had a lot of nerve, "come to my table. I'll be waiting on you."

I did not have to say anything. Peter took control. He had just won brownie points with me. I cannot deal with a man that will let anyone disrespect me.

"Hold up, Zeena. You know better than to stand here and disrespect my date. What we had is over." He pointed his finger back and forth between the two of them. "We really never had anything. We just fucked." He grabbed me by the hand, and we walked off. I turned and looked back at her. Her whole demeanor had changed. I laughed because baby girl had a whole new attitude now.

"I apologize," he said as we reached our table.

"It's all good. I ain't worried about her."

The waitress walked up to the table with a smile on her face.

"What's up, Black? Do you want your regular? A double shot of Patrón with a lot of limes?" She was a cute girl. She was very petite with naturally curly auburn hair. Her hazel eyes complimented her tan skin tone.

"Yes, that will be fine, Tiffany."

She turned and looked at me.

"What will you be having, sweetie?"

"Pineapple Cîroc will be fine for now. But before I decide about the food, let me look at the menu."

She pleasantly walked off.

"Is it safe to assume this is a regular spot for you?"

"Yes, it is. This place is relaxing. Please do not think I have been with all these women who are speaking to me. I'm just well known here."

"Oh, I don't let other people form opinions for me. I'll get my opinion of you from you." The waitress slid both of our drinks on the table. Finally, I was ready to order.

"I would like an order of twelve honey barbeque wings with a side of loaded fries." I looked up because I felt Peter looking at me.

"What?" I said in a joking manner.

"You gonna eat all that? Damn, woman, you *can* eat."

"Hush. I told you I had a fat-girl appetite."

"You got a fat girl beat." He busted out laughing. I had to laugh too. He was so stupid.

Kim

Since Keena was gone with Black, or Peter is what she called him, I decided to get up with Seth. I invited him over to the room. He should be here any minute. I turned the TV on while I waited for him. I had just settled on an oldie but goodie. *Good Times* was still my show. Then I heard a knock on my door.

"What's good, ma?"

I stepped aside and allowed him into the room.

"The game on, and you got the TV on *Good Times?*" He grabbed the remote before sitting on the bed, turned the TV to the game, and lay back on the bed.

It was halftime when Seth grabbed my leg and pulled me closer to him. He started rubbing his hand down it. Of course, I was asking for that. I wore a cute pair of red boy shorts and a white cami. My nipples were playing peekaboo through the thin material.

He looked me in the face as he slid off my boy shorts. "You got on too many clothes, ma." He took his thumb and pressed it against my pussy, then started rubbing it. I was biting my lip because it was starting to feel good. He then placed his lips on my pussy lips and began to suck slowly. I could hear the smacking noises because it was so loud. Soon, he pulled me to the edge of the bed as he got down on his knee. His tongue action was so magical that he had me screaming out in ecstasy. I felt his tongue flickering across my swollen pussy lips as I threw my body back toward him. I was trying to match his speed. It was feeling *that* damn good. Suddenly, he flipped me over, and my ass was all in the air. He scooted his face underneath me and continued to eat me out. My legs automatically started to shake.

"Damn, Seth. This shit feels *so* good." I started squirming.

"Lie down," he whispered in my ear. I did as I was told. He reached on the floor and grabbed a condom out of his pants pockets. After sliding it on that ten-inch anaconda, he pushed my legs back. First, he stuck it in slow. Then he sped up his pace. I tried to handle the dick, but he was long and wide.

"Let me get on top," I said out of breath. So I climbed on him and rode him rodeo style. He was holding my titties and was making circular motions on my nipples.

"Damn, Shonte."

I had almost forgotten that he only knew me as Shonte. I was about to act stupid on him. I was thinking he was calling me another bitch's name. I was slipping. I knew I had to stop getting high.

"Aww, fuck," we both yelled out in unison because we were both about to nut. Finally, when I got up, I saw the condom was coated with my juices.

He rose and walked to the bathroom. All types of thoughts were running through my mind. I honestly was not planning to sleep with him this soon. But, oh well, I don't stay here. I don't care about what he thinks.

Seth came back into the room with a warm wet rag for me. After we were done washing up, we lay down to finish watching the game. In the end, I fell asleep lying on his chest.

Chapter 18

Black

I must admit I had an enjoyable time with Keena. I was really feeling her. There was something about baby girl that I just could not leave alone. I even invited her to Sunday dinner. I knew that was a major step because not even Ebony had made it that far. I had never invited Ebony to a family dinner before. Not saying that I would not have, but we never made it that far. I did not want the day to end, but I could sense she was not ready for all that.

I pulled into my garage and shut off my engine. Then I walked into my foyer and shut off my alarm. As I took off my clothes, my phone went off, alerting me of a text message. I realized it was Keena. She was telling me she had a fun time and good night. I shot her a good night text back. I was exhausted and ready for bed. I hoped Zeena did not think I would let her get away with that little stunt she pulled at the bar. I was going to get in her shit about that. I thought about her name and Keena's name. It was uncanny how similar their names were. I made a mental note to call my mom and let her know about our addition to Sunday's dinner. Then I fell asleep with Keena on my mind.

I picked up my phone from the nightstand and looked at the screen. It was eleven thirty in the morning. I was running late to get my mom, so I called her to let her know I was on the way.

An hour later, I was pulling up to her house. The new neighbor Quan was standing outside by his car. I noticed the North Carolina tags, which is why I knew it was his car. I threw my head up at him, acknowledging his presence.

"What's up, Peter?"

"Not shit, man. Came to take Ma Dukes to the store, so she can get those pots jumping. A nigga be living for Sunday dinner."

"Yeah, I feel you."

We shared a laugh, and I walked in the door. I remembered I had forgotten to tell Paulina that Steven had asked about her.

"Yo, Paulina, that li'l nigga Steven asked about you. I forgot to tell you that the other day. Ma, are y'all ready?"

"Can you just go, Peter? Paulina don't want to leave the house yet."

Hearing my mom say that fucked me up in the head. No way my sister should feel like that.

"Oh yeah, Ma, before I forget, I invited Keena over for dinner."

"The lady that came to the hospital? The same one that was at the grocery store?"

"Yes, that's her, Ma," I said with a huge smile.

"She must be special because you don't bring nobody to my table."

I asked my mom what she wanted me to get from the store, then left.

Kim

I woke up with my legs twisted up with Seth's. I could not believe I had let him spend the night with me. I shook him to wake him up, but he did not stir. He looked so peaceful. His phone was buzzing. I wondered who was calling him. He was out all night, so I'm sure it was his girl trying to figure out why he didn't make it home last night. I'm not saying he has one, but hell, I do not trust niggas. I extracted myself from him because I had to pee badly.

When I came out of the bedroom, Seth was sitting on the bed, putting on his shoes. I had to admit I felt like a cheap whore watching him prepare to leave.

"So, you weren't going to say anything to me? You were just going to up and leave without a word?"

He looked up at me as if noticing me standing there for the first time.

"No, of course not." He stood up and walked toward me. He pulled me in for a hug. I could still smell his Gucci cologne. The scent was intoxicating. He kissed me on my cheek as he pulled away from me.

"I have some business to handle, though. I would love to take you out later tonight. How do dinner and a movie sound?"

Now, *that* put a smile on my face. "That sounds nice. Just let me know what time to be ready."

"I'll pick you up around seven."

We said our goodbyes, and he walked out the door.

Seth

As I drove down Sunset Boulevard, I had baby girl on my mind. I like her, but something about her seems off. I also feel like I have seen her somewhere before, but I cannot put my finger on it. I picked up the phone to call my boy Black. I had not heard from him in a while.

"What up, nigga?" I spoke as he answered the phone.

"Not shit, nigga. At the grocery store for Ma Dukes. Paulina refuses to leave the house, and you already know she ain't staying at the house by herself. I wish I could tell her that big brother handled that situation. She doesn't ever have to worry about those fuck boys anymore."

"Yeah, I feel you. Right now, she has no clue her big brother is a monster in these streets," Seth said with a chuckle in his voice. I joined in on the laughter.

"Man, I been kicking it with shorty from my birthday party. I even invited her to dinner today."

"Man, word? Yo, I cannot believe her mean ass is even talking to you. Shorty shot your ass down with the quickness. That shit was funny as hell."

"Man, shut the hell up. She did shoot me down, though. Man, she crushed me. I was not used to that shit."

"Man, I met a shorty too. I didn't mention it because you know I don't love them hoes." I busted out laughing at my own joke. Actually, I have never had a girlfriend. The streets were my girlfriend, and my money was my wife. This is the only life I knew. I did not have time for hoes. I would fuck them and throw them a few dollars, that's all. Then I was off to the next one. I did not have time for that clingy shit. A bitch will get you fucked up.

"Oh shit, nigga, you can't say shit about me. Let me find out. What's her name, nigga?"

"Shonte."

"Oh shit, every Shonte I know ghetto as fuck."

"Nigga, she ain't ghetto. You know I don't fuck with no ghetto-ass broads." We both were laughing. "Good, nigga. I was just calling to check on you. I did not want shit. Tell Ma Dukes I said what's up, and I will join y'all next week. I don't want to interrupt family time with your new boo."

"Man, go to hell with that."

"Right after you, nigga." I was laughing like hell as I hung up the phone. I always had to have the last word.

Keena

I looked at the time on my cell phone. It was almost time for Peter to pick me up. I called Kim because I needed to introduce her to Peter formally. Of course, he saw her at the grocery store, but he had not met her. I needed him to know who she was, so he could also relax around her. I was planning on being the distraction while Kim put in all the work. I was going to introduce her as Kim since he already knew my name. I told her to come to my room so we could go downstairs together.

Peter had just pulled up in his all-black Maserati as we walked out the door. His Forgiato rims were black as well. The only color on his car was his name, "Black" in silver scripted right above the gas tank. His windows were tinted with the mirror tint. That tint was illegal in North Carolina, even though that was my favorite tint. We walked toward his car as he hopped out to open the door. I could see the confused expression on his face. I quickly erased his confusion.

"Peter, this is my cousin, Kim. She came here from Georgia with me. Kim, this is Peter, but everyone calls him Black. You know me, though. I ain't everyone else, so, of course, I call him Peter." I looked over at Peter, and he was smiling.

"Nice to meet you, Kim." He grabbed her for a hug.

"Nice to meet you as well, Black." She spun on her heels to head back in as she yelled over her shoulder to have fun and let Peter know she had her eye on him.

“She is overly protective of me.”

“I see.”

When we pulled up to his mom’s house, a young boy and an older-looking version of him were outside next door playing basketball. I could tell he wasn’t his dad. Well, at least, he didn’t appear to be. He did not look old enough to be his father unless he had him very young.

I admired Peter’s mom’s house. It was made of a cement-type concrete material. It was a huge, two-story house. I couldn’t wait to see the inside. The neighbor walked over to us before we could get into the house.

He shook hands with Peter, and then he turned and looked at me. “Don’t I know you?” My heart started beating fast in my chest because he looked familiar too. I did not need him blowing my cover. Peter thinks I’m from Georgia.

“Nah, unless you from Georgia, you don’t know me.”

“I’m from North Carolina. Maybe you just look familiar.”

“Maybe I do. You know people say everyone has a twin.” As we were walking into his mom’s house, it clicked in my head where I knew him from. He got his hair cut in the same shop my hairstylist, Nina, worked. I just prayed he did not remember me.

When I say Peter’s mama’s house was laid, that would be an understatement. She gave me a tour of her house. Every room had its own theme. Her master bedroom was downstairs, and the other three were on top. Her dining room had a splash of orange and brown. An array of pictures decorated the place. I saw pictures of Peter hanging on the wall from his younger days. A massive picture of him and his parents hung over the fireplace.

"You have a lovely home, Ms. Jones."

"Thank you. Dinner is ready. I'll bring it out." Peter grabbed my hand and led me to the dining room.

Quan

Baby girl looked remarkably familiar. She says she's from Georgia, but I do not forget a face. I may forget a name, but never a face. Something is not right with that girl, but it ain't none of my business. I just met that nigga, so who am I to get all up in his business. I knew in due time I'd remember who she was.

Chapter 19

Black

A month later . . .

I had been kicking it with Keena for over a month, and I must admit, baby girl had me gone. My mom and my sister loved her. The only thing that bothered me was that my mom's neighbor, Quan, insisted that he knew her. I did not even know him, so that was strange.

It was Friday, and I knew King of Diamonds would be jumping. It was also All-Star Celebrity Friday so anybody could be in the building. I still had not met Seth's mystery woman. I was going to invite Keena, so I planned to tell him to invite Shonte. It would be nice for our ladies to get to know each other. Seth is my best friend, so it was only right that they knew each other. I dialed Keena first. I had to see how she felt about going to a strip club. Some women do not like strip clubs.

"Hey, baby," she answered the phone. I could hear that smile in her voice. I promise to always keep a smile on her beautiful face.

"I was just wondering how you felt about going to a strip club?"

"Am I going with you?"

"You know I ain't letting you go by yourself with all those thirsty-ass niggas."

She let out a little chuckle. "It can be a hundred niggas in that club, but I only got eyes for one, and that is you, my friend."

I must admit it stung a little bit when she called me her "friend." I could not be mad, though. We never really sat and talked about our relationship status. But I knew I had to make things official because I would act a fool if I saw her on another nigga's arm.

"Well, I know some women don't like to be in strip clubs, so I had to ask."

She flipped my statement back on me. "Do you think I'll let you be in a club full of thirsty women without me?"

"You don't have to worry about that. Well, I will invite Seth and his new significant other. I have not met her yet, so I'm anxious to see who's got my boy's nose wide open. He's been talking to her as long as I've been talking to you, and I have yet to meet her."

"Well, that doesn't sound right, being how close the two of you are."

"Our schedules just keep colliding, but that's why I'm inviting them. I want y'all two to meet as well. I'll pick you up around ten."

"That sounds fine to me." Then we hung up.

I decided to go check on my mom and sister. I had not seen them in two days. Of course, I talk to them every day, but I had not physically seen them.

When I pulled up, Paulina was on the porch talking to that damn boy, Steven, again. Whatever they were talking about had to have been very funny. She was showing all thirty-two of her pearly white teeth. I wasn't going to bother her about Steven because I had not seen her laugh so hard since she was raped. I thought back to the conversation with my mom. She told me my sister had to grow up sometime. I knew that, but it was hard to accept. Finally, she looked up and saw me getting out of my car. Her eyes got big as she walked off the porch toward me.

"Peter!" she said with so much excitement like she had not seen me in years.

"Hey, baby girl," I said as I rubbed her head. "What have you been up to?"

"I've been good, Peter."

We walked back toward my mom's house while we were talking.

"Have you decided when you want to go to Disney World?"

"I told Erica, but you will have to talk to her mom about it."

"That's fine," I said as I grabbed my mom and pulled her in for a hug.

"Where's my daughter-in-law?"

I looked at her kind of strangely.

"Don't be looking at me like that. You already know she's the one."

I could not help but smile. Keena had that effect on me. "We going out on a double date later with Seth. He's got this new chick he's been seeing for as long as I have seen Keena. I have never met her, so you know I gotta meet her. I need to see who's got my friend's nose wide open."

"Tell Seth he better get by here to see me. He's not been around in a while, and I want to meet this mystery woman too."

"OK, Ma, I'll let him know. I can't stay long. I just came by to check on y'all. I'll see you Sunday." I kissed her on her cheek and left.

Kim

My legs were wrapped around Seth's legs as I lay in his arms. We had been spending a lot of time together, and I loved every minute of it. Ashton would still text me every now and then, but I wouldn't respond, so I think he got the hint. No man had ever made me feel this damn good in a long time. Seth also had unlimited access to coke. He had so much of it that he did not even realize I was taking a little bit to feed my habit. Seth had a habit of keeping product where he lay his head. After taking me to his house the first time, I peeped where he kept his coke. I never took a noticeable amount, so he never knew. I must have been moving too much in bed because he opened his eyes and looked at me.

"What's on your mind, Sleeping Beauty?" he whispered in my ear.

"You are what's on my mind. I keep waiting to wake up from this dream."

"What dream are you talking about, ma?"

"This dream of us. I know I may be speaking too soon, but I'm loving the idea of us. I have never met a man like you before."

"That's because there's only one me," he said as he nibbled on my ear. His hand was now rubbing my titties as he sucked on my earlobe. I could feel the moisture in my panties as my pussy began to throb. Just from his touch alone, he had me gone. He had that kind of effect on me. I don't think he ever got tired of having sex with me. We went to bed having sex, which is how he wanted to wake up. I had no problem with that. I felt him ease my canary yellow thongs off my ass. He stopped before he pulled them down.

"What's wrong?" I asked him in a hushed tone.

"Nothing, ma. I was admiring how that ass just jiggles." He playfully slapped me on my ass, and I giggled like a schoolgirl. Then he stuck his middle finger in my pussy and pulled it out to taste it. This nigga was nasty, but I was feeling his nasty ass.

"Damn, ma, you taste good." He flipped me over on my back, spread my legs apart, and dived headfirst into my pussy. His tongue was lethal and should be registered as a deadly weapon. He had a long tongue like a snake's. I grabbed his head as he spread my pussy lips apart with his tongue. Then he licked my pussy up, down, and side to side like it was his last meal. He had me calling to heaven because that tongue had me gone. Next, he stuck his finger in my butt while he continued to lick me down. This shit was feeling so good I was lifting off the bed. Hell, I was running from his ass. He then flipped me over and started licking me from the back. He ran his tongue down the crack of my ass. It felt so moist. I put my ass in the air as I threw it back at him. He was tongue fucking me. I buried my face in the pillows to keep from screaming so loud, even though he stayed alone. Then I felt him ease his dick inside of me, and I prepared myself for it because his monster was *huge*.

"Aww!" I yelled out as he went in the first time.

He smacked me on my ass again as he thrust in and out of my pussy.

I started tightening my pussy muscles on his dick. I knew that would drive him crazy. It worked because I heard him let out a soft moan. I wanted to be in control, so I told him to lie down. I climbed on top of him as I slowly began to ride him. I grabbed both of his legs as a platform as I sped up my pace. Then I lifted my body up . . . and came back down. I was easing his dick in and out of my pussy as I looked him in his eyes. I wanted to see the look on his face as I fucked the shit out of him. The faces he made were priceless.

Chapter 20

Seth

I looked over at baby girl as she lay peacefully on her back. She had her phone in her hand as she scrolled Instagram. I was admiring her beauty when my phone went off on my nightstand. I was not into all those different ringtones, so I had to pick up my phone to see who was calling me. I noticed it was my nigga Black calling.

"What's up, nigga?" I said as I answered.

"Man, you know King of Diamonds will be jumping tonight. We ain't hung out in a while, so I was wondering if you and Shonte wanted to come out. Keena already said she was down with it."

"Word? She doesn't mind going to a strip club? I'm cool with it. I just gotta make sure my girl's cool with it too."

"Oh, she your girl now?" Black was laughing so hard at his own joke. "Don't think I missed your comment."

"Shut up, nigga. You heard what I said." I turned around and looked at Shonte.

"Do you want to join my nigga and his girl at King of Diamonds tonight?"

"Yes, that's fine with me." She got right back to messing with her phone.

"She says she's down, so I'll see you there later." We hung up the phone, and I turned to Shonte. "Are you really OK with going to a strip club?"

"Um, yes. Did not I say I would? So why are you asking me that again?"

"Many women don't like going to female strip clubs."

"I will climb a mountain as long as I do it with you."

That put a big-ass smile on my face.

Keena

I was mentally trying to decide what I would wear to the club tonight. I loved the condominium that we were renting. The walk-in closet was huge. The condominium was so spacious I would not even know if Kim was home. I missed the relationship that we had. We were not as close as we used to be. She had been spending a lot of time away from the house. I honestly do not know with whom or where she's been. She barely even talks to me. Like now, she was not even here, and I really needed to speak to my best friend. The feelings I had for Peter, a.k.a. Black, were unreal. He was my target. I was not supposed to be liking him. Slowly but surely, however, he was growing on me.

I heard my phone ringing. I reached for it as I noticed it was Joc calling. Usually, I'm happy to hear from him, but my feelings for him are not the same anymore.

"Hello."

"What's up, Keena? I was just checking on you. I hadn't heard from you in a while."

"I'm doing fine, Joc. You know how I am when I'm working."

He started laughing. "Oh, you're *working,* huh?"

"Shut up, Joc." I started laughing too.

"Well, I didn't want anything, for real. I was just checking on you, making sure everything was good on your end."

"It's just taking a little longer on my end. This nigga don't trust nobody."

"Well, let me know if you need me. I do care about you."

"I will." We both hung up. I felt kind of lousy lying to Joc like that. I didn't know how to tell him it was taking longer because I had second thoughts about it. I was starting to feel bad about setting Peter up.

I heard Kim come in the door because she was on her phone talking about going out tonight. It didn't matter because I had plans for tonight as well. I decided right then and there to speak with her later. It would not be tonight, though.

I lay across my king-size bed and grabbed my remote control, then started flicking the channels on my fifty-inch smart TV, trying to find something interesting to watch. Finally, I saw that *The Best Man* was on. I could watch that movie over and over.

I woke up to the ringing of my cell phone. It was Peter calling. I also noticed the time. It was after nine. I did not mean to sleep that long.

"Hello," I answered the phone all groggily.

"Hey, Sleeping Beauty. Did I wake you up?"

"Yes, you did, but I need to get up. I did not even realize it was this late. I went to sleep watching TV. What time are you coming to get me?"

"That's why I was calling you. Can you be ready around eleven?"

"Yes, I can. Let me get off this phone so that I can get dressed." I hung up.

I decided to wear my all-black Valentino maxi dress with one sleeve. It stopped midthigh, and my breasts were sitting up just right. I knew I had to shower quickly, but I decided to go to Kim's room to see what she was doing before I got in the shower. I wanted to let her know I was going out. Her door was wide open, so I knew she was already gone. Then I walked back to my room to bathe.

"Damn, you sexy as hell," Peter said as I opened the door for him. I turned all the way around to give him a full view. "Girl, you're going to make me hurt somebody up in the club tonight." I was blushing as I listened to him talk about me.

"You're too funny, Peter. Come on, so we can go."

Kim

I was up in the VIP section at King of Diamonds with Seth drinking it up. He had ordered a bottle of Belvedere Vodka, Grey Goose, Cîroc, Crown Royal, and two bottles of Patrón. We could serve the whole club with all the alcohol we had in our section. We were waiting on his homeboy and his girl to arrive. I really was not in the mood to meet anybody, but it was important to him. Since it was important to him, I made a sacrifice. He said his homeboy wanted to meet me. I was just trying to figure out why. I was dating Seth, not his homeboy. I needed to take a hit to get through this night, though, so I excused myself to the restroom.

I had just hit a line and was about to walk out of the stall when I heard some women mention Seth's name. I decided to stay in the stall a little longer to hear what they had to say.

"Did you see that bitch Seth walked in here with?"

"Yes, you know I saw that bitch. I can't believe he stopped fucking with me for her."

"Right. He could have at least upgraded because that bitch's ugly. He told me he was not fucking with me no more because he wanted to see how things went with her." I could not take it anymore, so I walked out of the stall.

"Bitch? Ugly where? Yes, he *did* upgrade. You look like a broke-down stripper with your run-over heels. He should have upgraded *your* ugly ass." Both of them had crazy looks on their faces. They did not expect me to be in the bathroom.

"Oh, cat got your motherfucking tongue now? Both of you had a million dollars' worth of words to say just a few minutes ago." At that moment, the bathroom door opened, and in walked Keena.

She locked eyes with me because I knew she was as shocked to see me as I was surprised to see her. I guess if I talked to her, neither of us would be shocked.

"Kim, what are you doing here?"

"Kim?" I heard the girl that used to mess with Seth ask. "I thought Seth said his new bitch's name was Shonte." I looked her in her face before I walked toward her. I got all up in her personal space. I needed to make sure she heard every word I was about to say.

"Listen here and listen here good. I am *not* going to be too many more bitches. Whatever you had with Seth is over. Get it through your head." By this time, I was pointing my finger at her face. "I heard you say it out your own mouth that he was not fucking with you."

"Whatever," she said as she threw her hands up and walked out of the bathroom. I felt Keena just staring at me. I knew she wanted to know who the hell the fight was over.

Seth was. I was in a whole life argument about him, so I knew I owed her an explanation.

Chapter 21

Keena

I listened to the conversation between Kim and those women and just knew my ears were deceiving me. This could *not* be the female that Seth was dating. I knew that it was, though. I knew Kim's fake name was Shonte. I heard them say Seth's girl's name was Shonte. I did not know what the hell to think or do. Peter had already met her as Kim. How the hell was I going to let him see her as Shonte? He would have so many questions. He knew we were not talking, so he would understand how I did not know who Seth was dating.

"Kim, please tell me you ain't dating Peter's best friend."

"I don't know who his best friend is, but I am dating Seth."

I guess a lightbulb must have gone off in her head suddenly. "Oh my God. *You* are Seth's homeboy's girl. He never said what her name was.

"Kim, how the hell are we supposed to walk back out there with Peter knowing your name is Kim and Seth knowing you as Shonte?"

"Hell, we'll just tell them Kimberly is my middle name. That way, Seth won't feel like I lied to him."

"Yes, that'll work. I don't know why I didn't think of that."

"You don't have to think of everything, Keena." She said that with an attitude in her voice. Silently, we both walked out of the restroom.

Black

I walked into King of Diamonds with Keena on my arm. She immediately had to rush to the bathroom. Women love flying to the bathroom to make sure they still look good. I just assumed she went to catch up with her cousin, Kim. I had just seen her walking toward the bathroom. I was trying to figure out why she was in VIP with Seth. That was not a good look on his part if he was trying to be serious about Shonte. I knew how Seth was, though. That's why I was so surprised that she had been around this long. Seth does not keep a female around too long. I walked over toward my nigga's section. I got stopped a few times on my way to the VIP by a few niggas, mostly females.

"What's up, my nigga?" Seth said as he stood up to give me a manly hug. I had not seen him in a while. Yeah, we talked on the phone, but I had not seen him physically.

"What's up, Seth?" I looked around before I spoke again. "Where's Shonte?"

"Oh, she went to the bathroom. You know how women do."

"True," I replied as I reached for a bottle of Patrón. I looked up as Keena walked up with her cousin Kim. I was shocked when Kim went and sat on Seth's lap. I thought that it was her I saw when we walked in, but I was confused. I really thought he was serious about Shonte.

"Peter, you remember my cousin, Kim," Keena said while she was pointing at her, but Seth had a puzzled look on his face. Kim started talking, trying to explain before Seth had a chance to say anything.

"Kimberly is my middle name, Seth. Keena has always called me Kim." Well, that eased my mind, I thought, because I was trying to figure out what was going on. I mean, Keena had mentioned that she hardly even talked to Kim these days. So I understood she may not have known that Kim and my boy were talking.

"I ran into Kim in the restroom and asked her what she was doing here. To my surprise, she said she was here with Seth. Now, ain't that funny?"

"So, let me get this straight. Y'all two *know* each other?" Seth pointed back and forth between Keena and Kim, or Shonte. "Whatever the hell her name is."

"Yes, Keena is my cousin."

"Why you never told me that?"

"How did I know to tell you? You never told me who your nigga was. You never said his name. All you ever called him was your nigga."

"Yeah, you're right. Well, at least I know y'all two will get along." He held his drink up in the air to gesture a toast. We all followed his lead.

I went over and paid one of the strippers to give Keena a lap dance. I didn't know how she would react, but it was all out of fun. I just wanted to see the reaction on her face.

I watched as the stripper walked over to her. "Black told me to dance for you." Keena threw her hands up, pushing the girl away.

"You're good, baby girl. You don't have to dance for me."

"I won't get my money if I don't dance for you."

I saw Keena lighten up some.

"Make your money then, baby girl." I watched Keena as the stripper started dancing. She was laughing and trying to make sure she did not get too close to her. We spent the rest of the night just laughing, drinking, and enjoying ourselves. Kim turned out to be cool as hell. I can tell

Keena enjoyed hanging out with her cousin. She laughed all night long.

Seth

To say I was shocked was an understatement. I did not know that Shonte, or Kim, whatever she wanted to call her damn self, knew Black's girl. But I'm happy that we all could get along because we all knew each other. Keena seemed pretty cool; I could tell Black was crazy about her. I had not seen that look in his eyes since Ebony. Even though he had not said it, I could see the love written all over his face. I just pray that Keena was one hundred because I will kill a bitch behind my best friend.

I noticed Shonte was drinking a little too much. I did not want to ruin the moment, but I could not stand a female who could not handle her liquor. As she reached over to pour herself another drink, I grabbed it out of her hand. She looked at me strangely, but I didn't care. We could have our first argument in public, but I was a man. She was going to respect what *I* said.

"What's up, Seth?" she said with her speech already slurring.

"I think you've had enough for one night." I thought she would go against what I said, but to my surprise, she didn't.

"Oh, OK, that's fine." She looked at her cell phone. "Seth, it's getting late. Can we go?"

I looked over at Black. He threw his hands up. "It *is* getting late, Seth. We can bounce."

Kim

I was mad as hell. Who the fuck did Seth think he was? He did not have a clue how badly I wanted to cuss his ass out. He ain't my damn daddy. I knew how much I needed this money, so I did not want to fall out with him. Then he had the nerve to question me about Keena. Hell, I didn't even know he knew Black. I thought back to the night of Black's party. That's why he looked so familiar to me. He was at that damn party. Well, at least everything is out in the open now. Keena's ass thinks she's slick. I know her better than she knows herself at times. I saw how she was looking at Black. She had nothing but love in her eyes. Shit, she better not forget the *real* reason we're here. This is a jackpot. She better forget about love. Hell, I was not about to let them fuck up my high.

I made up my mind that I was going to rehab once I got home. Then I would sit down and talk to Keena about my habit. I needed some support if I wanted to kick this. I looked over at Seth as he was pulling the car out of the parking lot. Apparently, he was talking to me, and I was not responding.

"What's up?"

"I asked you if you wanted to spend the night with me. What's on your mind?"

"Oh, nothing. I'm good. Yes, I'm spending the night with you."

He grabbed my hand and kissed it. "You are the truth, girl." He held my hand for the rest of the ride to his house.

Chapter 22

Black

We were on the way back to my crib. This would be the first time I took Keena to my house. We usually chill at her house or my mom's. I looked over at her. She had fallen asleep with her head on the window. I did not even ask her if she wanted to spend the night. This girl had my nose wide open and did not even know it. I prayed she was authentic because I did not want to kill her.

I was pulling into my circular driveway when she opened her eyes. "Where are we, Peter?"

"We're at my house."

"Your house?"

"Yes, my house."

"This is beautiful, Peter. What made you bring me to your house?"

"Well, we been kicking it, and I'm trying to take us to another level." I looked her in her eyes as I said that. She gave me that million-dollar smile that I love. Then she reached across the console and gave me a wet kiss on the mouth.

"Do you really mean that, Peter? You really want to be exclusive with me?"

"Yes, I do, for real. I had to admit to myself that I do have feelings for you. If it's okay with you, I want to be with just you." I looked over at her, and she had tears in her eyes. I reached over to wipe them away. “What’s wrong? Why are you crying?”

“You know I’m a virgin, right?” She laughed as she was saying it.

“Yes, I know that you are a virgin. You already told me that.”

“You still want me?”

“Yes, that makes it even better. I already know ain’t nobody else hit that but me.” I was softly poking her in between her legs as I was talking. “Come on, girl. Let us get out of this car.”

“Peter, this is beautiful,” Keena said as I was giving her a tour of my house.

“Well, you know my mom helped with the decorations.”

“I can definitely see your mom’s touch. She did a beautiful job.”

“I can’t wait to put some babies up in you. I can see a mini-me or two running around here.”

She threw up her hands. “Wait a minute. We’ve only been a couple for like thirty minutes.” We both started laughing.

“So, am I just jumping to conclusions?”

“No. I eventually want kids one day as well.”

“I saved the best for last.” I pushed open the French doors that led to my master bedroom. “This, my Queen, is where we’ll be sleeping.” I noticed she looked over at my beautifully decorated king-size bed. Then she looked down at herself.

“Peter, I don’t have any nightclothes. I didn’t know to bring any.”

“Don’t worry about it. I went shopping for you earlier. I got everything I thought you might need.”

“How did you know my size? Let me find out you been stalking me.” She was laughing at her own joke.

"Woman, ain't nobody been stalking you. I just pay attention to you." I walked to my huge walk-in closet, grabbed the bags I had for her, and then pointed at the bathroom.

I heard the shower water in the bathroom, so I decided to join Keena. I did not know how she would feel about it, but I was willing to take that chance. I took off my clothes and slid behind her in the shower. She turned her head around and kissed me on my mouth. I had my dick pressed against her back, and it was growing. She turned around and looked at me.

"Hmm," she said as she was pointing at my dick. "Why is your dick poking me in my back?" She had a sneaky grin on her face.

"Let me taste you, Keena. We don't have to have sex, but I do want to taste you." I saw how she was hesitant.

"I've never even had oral sex, Peter. All this is new to me."

"We can wait. I'm not rushing you."

"It's OK. I want to experience all those things with you."

"Are you sure?"

She nodded as she grabbed my hand and got out of the shower.

Keena

I don't know what I was thinking about when I led Peter out of the shower. I was scared out of my mind. I knew there was no turning back once I slept with him. I could no longer go with the original plan of robbing him. I had fallen for this man. He was my mark. I was not supposed to fall for him. I did not know how I would tell Kim and Joc that I no longer wanted to go through with this. I was in love with this man. There. I finally admitted it to myself. He was different. He reminded me so much of my father that it was scary. He treated me with so much respect and paid attention to me. It made me feel special when he told me he knew my size because he paid attention to me. I liked Joc, but he did not even make me feel like Peter had.

"What's wrong with you? Are you having second thoughts?"

"No. I'm scared. I will admit that, but I ain't having second thoughts."

"I promise, I will take my time."

I lay down on his 800-thread count Egyptian sheets. They were so soft. It felt like soft cotton on my skin. Of course, I was naked as the day I was born. I did not know what to do other than what I saw on TV. Peter reached over and dimmed the lights. He put his iPod on an old-school-type remix. When I heard "Freak Me" by Silk, I knew it was on.

"Relax," he whispered in my ear. He placed his tongue on the tip of my pussy, and I tensed up. I did not know what to expect. He started flicking his tongue back and forth. Then he started sucking on my pussy lips, and I lost my mind. I relaxed because it was starting to feel good. He was sticking his finger in my ass while eating me out. I was squirming because it felt so good. Then he swooped my ass up in the air while he was still eating me out, and I couldn't take it anymore. If his tongue was that good, I knew the dick would be even better. The sheets were wet under me, and to say I was embarrassed was an understatement. I guessed he sensed it because he said something.

"It's okay. You're supposed to do that." He grabbed his dick, and I already knew what was coming. His dick looked like a big ole anaconda. I started to panic. No way in the world that thing was going in me. He started rubbing the head of his dick against my pussy. I must admit it felt good. He then eased the head in.

"Ow," I yelled out. It was painful at first, and finally, it started to feel good. I relaxed and started enjoying it. Peter then pushed my legs back a little farther and sped up his pace. I was beginning to moan. The next thing I knew, my legs were shaking. I felt like I had an out-of-body experience. Then I felt his nut running down my leg.

"Aww, shit. Damn, baby, that was good. You know you're mine now, don't you?" I did not even answer his question. I was in love with this man. I didn't feel like any words needed to be spoken. I had just lost my virginity. The sad part about it is I did not have anybody to tell. My only friend acted like she hated me.

I looked up as Peter walked back into the room. He had a washcloth in his hand. He walked toward me and gently wiped my pussy. "You okay? How are you feeling?"

"I'm good. I don't have any regrets. I love you, Peter." I did not mean to say that aloud. I was so embarrassed because I didn't know if the feeling was mutual. It didn't make it any better when he didn't say anything. He just stared at me. I turned my head and closed my eyes. I didn't know how to feel. I heard him walking back toward the bathroom.

Once he got in there, he stuck his head back out the door. "Baby girl, I love you too." Then I felt so much better. I exhaled the breath that I was holding in. We made love the rest of the night.

Joc

Keena had been heavy on my mind. I saw a few pictures of her and Black on the King of Diamonds' Facebook page, but I didn't put too much thought into it. I knew she had to play her role. It was hard to get too close to Black. I was surprised she had made it that far. She wasn't the first female I had sent at him, but she was the only one I cared about. Years ago, I had sent Ebony at him. She had gotten close to him but ended up falling for that nigga. That's why I had her killed. Turk was my twin brother. I had a more personal vendetta against that nigga for killing my brother. Keena did not have a clue that this was personal to me. She never saw that side of me. I always treated her with the utmost respect. Little did she know once I got that call from her, I was going to kill Black.

Keena did not know I was born and raised in Miami. Actually, I don't know where she thinks I'm from. We never discussed that part of my life. I had recently gotten back from Miami. My nephew was murdered, and nobody even knew who killed him. I had asked around, but nobody had heard anything.

I knew Keena was about her paper. I didn't have to worry about her falling for that nigga. Her motto was always "fuck niggas and get money." Once she was done in Miami, I was going to wife her. There was something about her that I just could not shake. Yes, I was older than her, but that didn't mean anything. I knew she robbed niggas for a living, but that didn't faze me. She wanted out just like I did. She was the one I wanted to settle down with.

I grabbed my phone and shot her a text message. I let her know I was thinking about her and to call me when she woke up. It was late, so I wasn't expecting her to respond tonight.

Seth

I looked over at Shonte as she lay on her side peacefully sleeping and laughed at the sight of the little drool on her face. She was slightly snoring. I wrapped my arms around her and pulled her in closer to me. I was really feeling the hell out of her, but something about her was off. The street side in me just would not let that go, but I could not put my finger on it.

She opened her eyes and looked at me. "Why are you watching me sleep, Seth?"

"I was just thinking about how amazing you are." I kissed her on her forehead. I wanted to make love to her. I could not get enough of her. She felt so good to me. I turned her around and slid up in her. She tooted her ass out to give me better access. I slid in slowly and then pulled out. As I sped up the pace, I slapped her on her ass. She rolled over and got on all fours. I got behind her and started pounding in and out of her.

"Ugg," she screamed. "Damn, Seth." She was throwing that phat ass all on my dick. I watched as my dick went in and out with her cum all over it. That shit was driving me crazy. I felt my nut building up at the tip of my head. Then I grabbed her by the waist and held her in the air. I was fucking her hard and fast as she was screaming out my name. Finally, I brought her down hard on my dick as I released all my seeds up in her. It was at that moment that I realized I was not wearing a condom.

The next morning, I took Shonte to Walgreens to get a morning-after pill. It's not that I did not want any kids. I just did not want any right now. I did not believe in abortions, so this was a sure way to stop it. She did not seem to have a problem with it. But if she did, she didn't say anything. I decided to ask her anyway just so there would be no bad vibes between us.

"Are you OK? You haven't said a word."

"Yes, I'm OK. Why wouldn't I be?"

"I don't want you to feel like I don't want a child with you. I'm just not ready for that right now."

She blew air out of her mouth before she spoke again. "We cool, Seth."

Then we rode in silence the rest of the way to my house.

Chapter 23

Kim

I honestly did not have much to say to Seth at the moment. I am not ready for a baby right now, but I did not like how he handled the situation. He did not even discuss this with me. He pretty much woke me up out of my sleep and said, "Come on." I didn't even know where we were going until we pulled into the pharmacy parking lot. He told me what we were there for when we arrived. I would have agreed with him if he had just asked. The fact that he did not had me looking at him differently. I felt like he was trying to handle me. Finally, I decided to say something to him about it. If I let this go, it will only get worse. I turned down the music in the car. I wanted him to know I was serious about what I was about to say.

He turned to look at me before he glanced back at the road. We were pulling into his garage by this time anyway. "Seth, you didn't have to handle me like I'm some random ho. I agree with you about not wanting a baby right now. But you did not even think to discuss this with me. Instead, you woke me up out of my sleep and made demands."

"You know what, Shonte? You're right. I have to respect what you just said. You're definitely not just some random chick, and I should have respected you more than that. I didn't mean to have raw sex with you, but it happened so fast." He reached over and grabbed my hand. "Do you forgive me?"

"Of course, I do."

We both got out of the car.

Keena

I saw the text message from Joc, but I never responded. I thought I liked him up until now. I did want us to remain friends. I knew I would have to tell him something, but I didn't know when. All I knew was I was not going to tell him now. I would not be disrespecting Black, so it would be soon. I saw Black looking over my shoulder as I read the text and saw the bewildered look he had on his face. I knew I owed him an explanation. Finally, I turned to look at him.

"I am *not* in a relationship with Joc. I will admit he likes me, and the feeling was mutual until I met you. I never went out with him, and we never shared more than a hug. I have talked to him a few times since I've been here, but I do not want to disrespect you, which is why I'm telling you this. I know I owe him an explanation, but I didn't want to go behind your back talking to him."

"I do appreciate you for keeping it real with me. I knew you was the one." He was laughing as he was talking. Then he grabbed me and held on tight. "Handle your business, baby. I trust you."

"Peter, can you take me home a little later?"

"You trying to leave me? I was hoping I could get some more of that good stuff you got between your legs."

I playfully pushed him. "Is that all you want from me?"

"Yep," he said as he ran out of the room. I ran right behind him.

His house was made in a circle. He had two sets of stairs, one on each side of the house. He took off up the steps. He thought I was going to go up them too. I tricked him, though. I ran up the other set and met him in the middle. He tackled me to the floor and started kissing all over me.

"You're cheating, Peter." I was laughing the whole time. I swear, it seems like I have known this man a lifetime. My first time ever having sex with him or having sex, period, and I could not get enough. We ended up having sex right there on the staircase.

I ended up taking one of Peter's cars home. He probably wanted to make sure I was coming back. I needed to talk to Kim. I was tired of us going around like nothing was wrong. As I walked into our condo, I realized I should have called her first because she was not at home. I walked into her room to see if there was any sign that she had stayed the night. I knew she stayed with Seth, but I wanted to check anyway.

As I was walking out of her room, something caught my attention out of the corner of my eye. It was a small bag on her bathroom counter that glistened from the sun. I returned to the bathroom and quickly realized it was a drug bag. *What in the world is Kim doing with this? We don't mess with that shit. I always sell any drugs we get to Joc.* Then I noticed the powder residue on the counter. *Oh, hell no.* Tears immediately filled my eyes. I did not want to believe my best friend was snorting powder. How did I miss the signs?

I knew something was not right. When did life become that hard for her? It hurt even more that she felt like she could not come and talk to me about it. Knowing my best friend, I realized she was too ashamed to say anything to me. She should have known I would not judge her. I immediately picked up my phone and started calling Kim back-to-back, but she would not answer my calls. I needed answers. I needed to know what was going on with her. Why would she stoop to drugs?

I sat in the middle of her bathroom floor and cried for what seemed like hours. Peter was calling me. I didn't even want to talk to him. I let all his calls roll to voicemail. I was hurt. I felt like I had failed my best friend.

Black

I had been calling Keena for hours with no response. All kinds of thoughts were running through my head. I could not go through this again. It finally clicked in my head that she was driving my car. I knew I was tripping because I should have thought about this hours ago. I picked up my phone and immediately dialed OnStar. Once they gave me the location, I realized she was at her condo. I grabbed my .380 and my .45 and ran out the door.

When I pulled up to Keena's condominium, I saw my car parked right beside hers. I walked up to her door, but it was locked, so I started beating on the door. I was hitting so hard that her nosy neighbor came out of her condominium.

"Sir, if you don't leave, I'll call the police."

I assumed she saw my gun because she immediately went back to her spot. Then finally, Keena opened her door.

"Peter, what are you doing here?"

"What do you mean what am I doing here? I've been calling your ungrateful ass for hours with no damn response." I knew I had an attitude, but fuck that shit. I was scared. She placed her hand over her chest. I knew she was shocked to hear me talk to her that way. I calmed down once I saw how puffy her eyes were. I immediately grabbed her. "What's wrong with you? What's going on? Please, don't cry." She started crying on my shoulder. I ushered her back into her condo and listened as she told me what she had discovered.

I don't know how I missed that. Probably because I had not been around Kim to notice it. Seth was around her every day. He's a real street nigga. He sells this shit. How did *he* miss it?

"We're going to help her. Just talk to her to see if she wants help. I promise you, money is not a problem. I'll pay for the best rehab around."

"I've *been* calling her. She won't answer her phone."

"Grab whatever you're going to grab. I'll follow you back to my house." I was already planning to take her out tonight, but I now knew she *really* needed to get out of here. We were going to Club LIV, so I told Keena to get dressed.

I watched as she tried to reach Kim again with no luck. I was going to have to holla at Seth about that because Keena was tripping. Finally, Keena decided to get dressed.

We were upstairs at Club LIV in the VIP area. We could see down on the dance floor and were enjoying our view. I loved the vibe of this club. It had a mixed crowd. We watched as the different couples danced off the various songs that the DJ spun. I grabbed Keena and pulled her in for a dance as the DJ played the remix of "Love" in this club by Usher, Lil Wayne, and Beyoncé. I actually liked that song. To my surprise, Keena was a wonderful dancer. I swear, as we danced, I felt like we were the only people in the club. We danced straight through the next three songs.

One of the bartenders came by and handed us a few Jell-O shots. Then the club photographer came by and took a few pictures. I made sure to buy one for me and one for Keena. I was really having a fun time. I could tell her mind was at ease, at least for the moment. She looked over at me and smiled. That was all I wanted to see. That smile made my night. I don't know where Keena came from, but I was glad to have her in my life.

Kim

I saw that Keena kept calling me, but I didn't answer the phone because I didn't want to talk to her. I did enjoy her company, and honestly, I missed her, but I did not like being around her. Keena knew me like the back of her hand. That's the reason I avoided her. But I wanted to talk to her about what was going on with me. In my heart, I knew that she would not judge me. I wanted my friend back. She was all I had.

It was late, and Seth was asleep. I had already dipped inside his stash. I needed a hit bad. I had been waiting all night for him to go to sleep. I had to fuck him really good to tire him out. Suddenly, I jumped at the sound of my cell phone buzzing. I knew I was just paranoid. I have never been around Seth this long. Typically, by now, I would have had some space. I saw that it was Ashton sending me a text message. I guess he just didn't give up. I had not responded to the last three text messages. I assumed by now that he would have gotten the message. Since he had just sent me a text message, it let me know he had not. I hit the delete button to erase the message and laid my phone back down.

All I wanted was a little hit before I went to bed. Tonight was my last night getting high. I went into the guest bathroom because I didn't want to be interrupted. Just in case Seth woke up and had to use the toilet. I wanted to enjoy my high in peace.

I emptied the package onto the bathroom counter, pulled out a small straw, inhaled one line, and then another one. After that, I sat down on the toilet because the room started spinning, and my chest was hurting. I could hear my heart beating through my chest. It was beating so hard. In fact, I thought it was about to explode. The next thing I knew, I saw my mom's face. She was reaching for me, but she had a disappointed look on her face. It was a look of shame. I just held my head down. I was afraid to look at her.

Do not look down now, Kimberly. What are you ashamed of? I know I did not raise you like this. But as hard as life was for me, I never turned to drugs.

It is just hard, Mama. I didn't choose this life.

You are stronger than this, Kimberly. I need for you to fight. You have to kick this habit.

She started to slip away. I was calling her name, but it was falling on deaf ears. My chest was hurting worse now than it was before. I knew I was having a heart attack, and nobody was there to help me. I had locked myself in the guest bathroom on the other side of the house. Seth would not be able to hear me even if I hollered out for help. I did not want to die this way. I did not want to be alone and die from an overdose.

I did not have a clue that this was going to be my last hit. Little did I know the coke that I took this time was pure and uncut . . . and my heart could not take it.

Seth

I woke up, and Shonte was not next to me. For real, her vacant spot is what woke me up. I had gotten so used to her lying in bed beside me that I was reaching for her. I looked toward my bathroom and noticed the light was off. I knew she was not in there, sitting in the dark. Maybe she went to the kitchen, I thought to myself as I reached for my remote control.

I was on my second commercial when I realized she still had not returned. *What is this damn girl doing?* I thought to myself. I jumped up from my bed, naked as the day I was born, dick swinging and all. Hell, it ain't like she never saw it before. I was going to put it on her ass again once she returned to bed.

I walked down the stairs to the kitchen and noticed she was nowhere to be found. She was not down here at all. I thought back to earlier. Was she more upset than she let on to be? Would she just up and leave without telling me or even waking me up?

I returned upstairs and noticed her purse was still there, so that meant she was still in the house. I let out a sigh of relief. Then I walked down the upstairs hallway and noticed the bathroom door was closed. I figured she was in there because I don't normally shut that door. Either way, she'd been in there a long time, so I knocked on the door, but she did not say anything.

"Shonte, open this damn door. What the hell are you doing in there?" Still, there was no response. "Shonte, don't make me break down this damn door." Something was not right. I had to get in there. I was not prepared for what I found on the other side of the door, though.

Shonte was lying on the floor, unresponsive. I started doing CPR on her. I was caught in a dilemma because my phone was in my room, and I knew I needed an ambulance.

I ran to my room and grabbed my phone. I started explaining to the 911 operator what was going on. They were trying to tell me different things to do.

"Can y'all just hurry the fuck on? Damn."

I heard her saying to calm down because she was trying to help me. I did not want to hear that shit. I surveyed the bathroom and saw why Shonte was lying on the floor. I could not believe this shit. How in the hell did I miss this? I kept saying something was off with her, but I was not expecting this. I usually can spot a dope fiend. I guess I was blinded by love. I got up so I could get rid of the evidence. I did not need those nosy motherfuckers all up in my business, especially doing what I do. I also had to put some clothes on because I was still naked.

I ran downstairs to let the firefighters in. I had heard the sirens outside. I learned that firefighters always come before the paramedics because they have more training. I always thought that was odd.

The paramedics were right behind the firefighters. I watched while they worked on Shonte. One of them was asking me a bunch of questions. I gave them her full name or what I thought was her name. It was not looking good. With my keys and cell phone in my hand, I followed behind the ambulance. I knew I would have to call Black so he could let Keena know, but I wanted to make sure Shonte was good first and find out which hospital they were taking her to.

We were headed toward Ryder Trauma Center. Damn, why did this girl have to be a powder head? The crazy part is I still wanted to be with her. I was willing to help her kick this habit. Just save her, Lord, please. I know I do not pray as I should, but I need you now, Lord.

I pulled up in front of the emergency room, right behind the ambulance. I dared somebody to say anything about my car. The paramedics were still working on her as they were getting her out of the ambulance.

Joc

I was lying across my bed scrolling my Facebook page. I had Keena on my mind. I was wondering what she was doing now. My Facebook scrolling was interrupted by the ringing of my telephone. I saw it was one of my homeboys from Miami.

"What's up?" I spoke into the phone as I looked out of my bedroom window. Nobody knew where I stayed. They probably thought I stayed at the trap.

"I found out who killed your nephew."

I perked up at the sound of that. I had been asking around, and this was the first lead I had. I was not ready for the answer he gave me, though.

"Black killed your nephew."

"Wait a minute. I'm confused. What do you mean Black killed my nephew?"

"Hey, I'm just telling you what I found out."

"Black had no reason to even come after my nephew. Li'l Turk's not even on his level." This did not make any sense. I cannot stand Black, but I had to admit, he does not bother anybody. You have to do something to him for him to come after you.

"Well, word on the streets is Li'l Turk and his friend kidnapped and raped his sister. I mean, Joc, I hate your nephew dead, man, but rape? He violated all kinds of codes. I have no respect for a rapist, and she was only 13 years old, man."

This shit had me bugging the fuck out. What was Li'l Turk thinking? I agreed with my nigga. He did not have to rape her. I wondered why he would do such a thing. I know my questions would go unanswered because he was dead. I still had to get at that nigga, though. My nephew was wrong, but still, Black killed him. For *that,* he had to pay.

"Thank you for the information, Cam." I hung up the phone. I did not want to hear anymore.

I continued to scroll my Facebook. I was scrolling so fast that I almost missed it. I had to scroll back up. One of my homegirls from Miami took a selfie at Club LIV. I had to blow up the picture to make sure I was seeing it right. Yes, it was Keena and Black in the flesh. I went through all the photos my homegirl had taken at the club. Keena and Black were in quite a few of them. Some of them were kissing and dancing. Keena looked like she was enjoying being around him. I was furious right now. All I saw was red.

I picked up my phone and started calling her number. Of course, she didn't answer. She was somewhere all in that nigga's face. I realized right then and there that my feelings were deeper for her than I thought. Since she would not answer the phone, I started sending text messages. I should have known better than to send a bitch to do a man's job. I went online to find a flight. I was going to Miami.

Black

I was lying across the bed watching *Bad Boys II* with Will Smith and Martin Lawrence. Gabriel Union was my baby. Keena was in the shower, and her phone was getting on my nerves. Now, I'm not that nigga to pry. I ain't no bitch-ass nigga, so I don't just be snooping in her phone. But whoever it was, I assumed really wanted something. As soon as the phone quit, they would call right back.

I got up to go to the bathroom. "Keena, your phone is about to drive a nigga crazy. Get out of the shower so you can answer it. It may be important."

"Peter, I am not interrupting my shower to talk to nobody. They can wait, or better yet, just answer it."

"I ain't answering your phone. It may be that nigga, and I do not want to have to fuck him up. What happened to him anyway? Did you get a chance to talk to him yet?"

"No, I haven't talked to him yet, but I will."

"Yo, you need to handle that shit. I don't understand what the holdup is. You say you love me, so dead that shit, Keena."

I walked out of the bathroom and went to the kitchen to get something to drink. When I returned to the room, her phone was still going off. Only this time, it was text messages. I picked up her phone only because she said I could. I was going to turn it off, but my street intuition would not let me. I saw that all her missed calls and text messages were from that nigga Joc.

After reading the text messages he sent, I could not believe my eyes. I had to go back and reread them. I could not believe this shit. I actually loved this bitch. No—scratch that. I was *in love* with this bitch. I trusted her, something I do not normally do. I had this snake-ass bitch around my family. As much as I loved her, I hated to have to kill her, but I had to. She betrayed me. Trust was big to me. The business that I was in made you be careful. I reached under my mattress and grabbed my .357 Magnum. Then I sat on my bed facing the bathroom with my gun in my hand. I was going to give her a chance to explain herself because all I wanted to know was *why*. Finally, the shower shut off.

Keena

That shower gave me life. I had my Plies bumping throughout the speakers that Peter had surrounding the bathroom. That song kept it real is the truth. I was putting on my Victoria's Secret Pure Seduction Lotion while rapping the chorus.

"I broke bread with you nigga, showed you where I live. You talk it, nigga, but you don't understand what real is."

I was in my zone. Plies killed the whole game with that one song. That is exactly how I felt. I wondered, though, who kept calling me. In my heart, I knew it was Joc. I knew I had to talk to him sooner than later. I no longer had the heart to keep the plan in motion. I have fallen in love with Peter. I could see us getting married and having some kids.

When I walked out of the bathroom, I was taken aback by Peter sitting on his bed with a gun in his hand. He had a crazed look on his face. I stopped dead in my tracks as

I noticed my phone was lying beside him. All that was going through my mind was that he had found out. I did not know what to do or think. I knew he had to have seen a text message. Kim would not text anything like that, so it had to have been Joc.

"Do you have something you need to tell me?" He was pushing my phone toward me. "So, all of this was a lie? You were sent here to set me up?"

Tears had started to roll down my face. I never meant for him to find out. This was all my fault. I should have said something to Joc.

"Nah, bitch, don't cry now. I bet you and that nigga Joc got a good laugh off me."

"Peter, please, let me explain."

"Bitch, don't say my name. I know my motherfucking name." He wiped his face. I saw a lone tear fall. I realized that he, for real, had fallen for me, and I had hurt him. That broke my heart. I reached out to touch him, but he slapped my hand down. "Bitch, don't you fucking touch me. You are a snake, and I hate the day I ever met you."

"Peter, please, listen. Yes, it was a setup at first, but I changed my mind. I couldn't go through with it."

"*Why* couldn't you go through with it, Keena? Tell me."

My lips were quivering as I was trying to speak.

"I fell in love with you, Peter. I fell in love. You are different. I did not expect to fall for you. This is my life, my hustle. Yes, I own everything I told you about, and setting people up is how I get my money. Only this time, it was different. You showed me a whole new way of life. For the first time since my daddy died, other than Kim, you showed me love."

"Keena."

That is all he said. He did not say anything else as he looked at me. It's like time was at a standstill. Then, out of the blue, he picked up his sixty-inch TV and threw it against the wall. "Damn, Keena. This shit right here hurts." He pointed to his chest. "You know I love you, right, but I got to kill you. I no longer trust you."

I saw him reaching for his gun. "No, Peter. You do *not* have to do this. I'll just leave, and you don't ever have to hear from me again." He lifted his gun and pointed it at me. I ran toward him just as the gun went off. I was not hit, so I let out a sigh of relief. I was trying to get the weapon away from him. I heard the gun go off again. It was so close to my ear that it was deafening. My ears were ringing, and I felt like I was losing consciousness. I looked down, and all I saw was blood. Blood was all over my pajamas. I said a quick prayer. I looked at Peter; he also had blood all over him. All I heard was the ringing of the doorbell before I passed out.

Chapter 24

Kim

I woke up to a bunch of beeping sounds and tubes running everywhere. I saw Seth sitting on the couch by the window. He was giving me a sinister stare. I was willing him to say something, I mean, anything, with my eyes. It was as if I had lost my voice. He never spoke. He only came over to the bed and placed a small kiss on my forehead, then walked out of the room. Shortly after that, a nurse walked into my room, with the doctor following shortly after.

"Well, Ms. Williams, you gave us quite a scare. I've been medicating you with Suboxone to help wean you off the cocaine we found in your system. Do you even know why you are here?" I shook my head. I slightly remembered, but that's all. "Well, you were brought in on a drug overdose. You're lucky even to be alive."

Tears started to roll down my face. I thought back to the dream I had about my mom. I knew she would be disappointed in me. Hell, *I* was disappointed in myself. I cannot even believe I let myself get to this point. As the doctor was talking, Seth walked back into the room. I wondered where he had been. But I did not have to think long because I noticed a white Styrofoam box in his hand. I also smelled the aroma of food. My stomach immediately started growling. It was a very loud noise, and I looked at him to see if he had noticed. I was so embarrassed, but it did not seem to bother Seth at all. I wondered when was the last time I ate anything. I'm sure food was the last thing on my mind because all I was worried about was getting high.

The doctor said a few more things, and then he left the room with the nurse following right behind him. They said some medical talk that sounded like a foreign language, but I did not want them to leave. I was afraid of being alone with Seth at the moment. I'm not sure if it was fear or I was too ashamed to face him.

"Do you have something you need to talk to me about?" he said as he moved the recliner closer to the bed. I shook my head no because I was confused about what he was talking about.

"I found you on my bathroom floor. You need to be telling me something."

I reached for the button to raise the pillow. I wanted him to know I was telling him the truth about what I was about to say. I began to tell him my story about what Bone had done to me. The only part I left out was how he died. If I told him that part, I would have to tell him how his best friend, Black, was our target. I could not tell him that because he would surely kill Keena and me. Speaking of Keena, I wondered if she even knew I was here. Seth just stared at me. He did not say anything. I don't know if he was waiting on me to say something else. Finally, he broke the silence.

"So, where is this fuck nigga at? I'm going to kill him."

"I don't know where he's at. I have not seen him since."

"What kind of real nigga would do some fuck shit like that? I mean, I have no respect for a nigga like that. Do you want to be clean?"

I nodded my head as the tears developed again. I was tired of crying and tired of feeling sorry for myself. I knew I had to do better. Hell, I *wanted* to do better.

"I'm so ashamed. I always thought I was stronger than that. I don't know how I became so weak."

"That doesn't make you weak. That nigga should not have done that to you. If you want help, I will help you. I fell in love with you, so I can't just turn my back on you."

"Does Keena know I'm in here?"

"No. I've been trying to reach Black, but I can't seem to get him on the phone. I don't know what's going on with that." He reached for his phone and dialed a number. I assumed he was calling Black again. I watched as he blew air out of his mouth. I knew then that he indeed was trying to reach him, and again, he had no luck.

Chapter 25

Keena

I watched as the hospital staff tried to revive Peter. That was the second time that he had coded. He had already undergone emergency surgery. I was in panic mode. The police were getting on my last damn nerve, and I did not have his mom's number. I did not want to leave the hospital because I did not want him to be left alone. Anything could happen on my drive to his mom's house. I wanted to be the first face he saw when he woke up. I had to have faith. It was not supposed to end like this. I had fallen in love with Peter. He was the first man I had ever loved outside of my dad. I did not love Joc. I had a strong like for Joc, but love I did not.

Beep! Beep! I heard the machine as Peter's heart started back beating. I let out a long breath that I did not even realize I was holding. The footsteps behind me instantly grabbed my attention, causing me to turn around. The detective that was assigned to the case was walking up to me.

"Ms. Jackson, I hate to do this to you, but I have to place you under arrest for attempted murder. We do not know what happened. I know you said it was self-defense, but you are not from here, and we need to get to the bottom of this."

The tears I had been holding back automatically started rolling down my face. I thought back to all the things that I had done in life. So many things I should have been arrested for, but I was not. Now, I'm being arrested for something I did not even do. This was one of the most heartbreaking events I had been through. I did not want to leave Peter here by himself. I knew I would go crazy worrying about him.

I barely heard the officer as he Mirandized me. My head was throbbing, and my vision was becoming blurred. All I could think about was Peter. He would wake up alone and wonder how he ended up there. I thought back to what happened. Peter and I wrestled for the gun when it went off. I did not mean to shoot him. However, I did not want to put Peter under investigation either. Therefore, I did not know how to handle the slew of questions I knew was coming. On the way down the long, dreary corridor, I saw Seth. I immediately got excited because I knew that Peter would not be alone. I was happy that Seth had somehow got word that he was in the hospital, but my happiness was cut short once he yelled.

"Keena! What the hell is going on? I've been blowing up Peter's phone up all day."

I knew he only used Peter's first name just in case the police had heard of the infamous Black. The name "Black" was well known, but they could never pin anything on him. They did not have a clue who Black even was. Peter was always careful in everything he did. Seth did not want to tie them together.

I blurted out as much as possible without incriminating myself before the officer pulled me along. "I'll be down there to see what's going on. Let me call his mom."

Hearing Seth say he was calling Peter's mom was music to my ears. I also had mixed emotions about it because it could be a blessing as well as a curse. It was a blessing because I knew she would rush to be by his side. I knew he would not wake up alone. The curse part is explaining why the police feel like I tried to kill her son. I knew I had a lot of explaining to do, but I did not feel like doing it now. So I was just going to stick with my story. It was not a lie, but it was not exactly the whole truth.

Hours later, I was walking out of the Fifth Precinct in Miami, Florida. I felt nasty and disgusted. They questioned me for hours, and I felt like it was a waste of my time. All I wanted to do was go home and take a long hot shower. I wanted to wash all the filth off me that I felt like I had picked up at that nasty-ass jail. The funny part is none of the questions they asked had anything to do with the actual shooting. Instead, they wanted to know what I knew about Peter. Apparently, he had been under their radar, but they could never find enough evidence on him. He moves in silence, is all the detective kept saying to me. I didn't know what they wanted from me. They had also brought Seth's name up and showed me all the pictures of them with different women. I guess that was supposed to get me to sing like a bird. They just did not know I was not an average bitch. I was not even a jealous bitch. Those women were before me anyway. Even if they were not before me, I still would not have said anything.

Cops always try to use some leverage with a woman that they think will work. I do not have any kids, so they had to stoop to the level of trying to have me feeling like I was being cheated on. I hated cops. Right now, all Black people hate cops because they are killing our race. Not only were they killing us, but they were also getting away with it too.

They also wanted to know if I had heard of a dude name Black. I laughed to myself when they asked me that, but I kept a poker face when I looked the detective in the eyes and told him no. Dumb-ass cop better find him a dummy because I am *not* the one.

They ruled it self-defense because they saw the bruises on my body. They also gave me information about a battered women's shelter. They kept asking me how I could be with a man that would put his hands on me. Of course, they did not know the whole story. That's why I never paid them any attention. Peter would never put his hands on me. That nasty-ass detective made sure he told me they would be in touch. I was not bothered at all.

I looked up as I heard a horn blowing and someone calling my name at the same time. I knew it could not be anybody but Seth because I did not know anybody else in Miami. I walked toward the car and got in. Unfortunately, I knew that my long-awaited shower would have to wait.

"What's up, Seth? Thank you for coming to get me. Where's Kim? I mean Shonte." I had to fix it because he gave me a weird look. I know he knew her name was Kim, but she introduced herself to him as Shonte.

He got quiet before he started talking to me. "Did you know your girl was getting high?" I put my head down. I felt guilty, even though I had just found out my damn self. I still felt like I had let her down. I'm supposed to be my sister's keeper. "I'm taking that as a yes. So, do you get high too? They say birds of a feather flock together."

I turned around and glared at him. "No, I do *not* get high. I just found out that she got high yesterday. I went home, and she was not there. I went to her bathroom, and that's where I found the powder residue. I was heartbroken when I found out. I cried out to Peter. I was in a daze when I found out and blocked out Peter. He was calling my phone, looking for me. When I didn't answer, he came to my condo looking for me, and that's when he found me on the bathroom floor crying like a baby."

"She overdosed last night."

I thought my heart was going to burst. It was beating so loud you could hear it inside of the car. No way could I lose Kim. We are not seeing eye to eye right now, but she *is* my sister.

"They were able to stabilize her. She's fine. What happened to my nigga, though? His mom and sister are at the hospital with him right now. He's in a coma." I was trying to figure out what to say to him without telling on myself.

"I was supposed to close a chapter in my life that I didn't close." I began to tell Seth my story as we drove to the hospital. "The guy kept calling and texting my phone, and Peter and I got into it about it."

"It got that bad where he pulled out a gun on you? That is *not* how Black operates. He would not shoot you over no boyfriend-girlfriend beef. So what are you *not* telling me?"

"He said I hurt him, and he could no longer trust me. I didn't know if he was going to shoot me. All I know is he had the gun in his hand, so I got scared." He nodded his head and continued to drive.

"My nigga in a coma, so I have no way of checking your story. But I know he loves you. I do not know what went wrong between the two of you, but for now, I will let it ride. Your girl and my nigga are in the same hospital. So, let's just get through this together."

We rode in silence the rest of the way to the hospital.

Chapter 26

Joc

I had just touched down in Miami and was walking through baggage claim, checking out the scenery. A car was waiting for me when I stepped out that door. The sun was beaming down, and I had to place my hand over my face to shield it from the sun. In a way, I missed this weather. There was no place like home. I inhaled the air, and it smelled like saltwater. This heat was so hot it was boring through my skin as beads of sweat dripped down my face. It was not this hot in Charlotte. This weather was more humid here. I checked the weather on my phone and noticed the temperature was ninety-eight. That explained the sweat on my body.

I pulled my car on Biscayne Bay as I headed to my condominium in downtown Miami. I was in love with the view that this area provided. I picked this condominium especially for this reason alone because I had a front-row seat from my penthouse on the sixth floor.

I walked through the door and over to my jaw-dropping view of Biscayne Bay. Every room in my penthouse had a fantastic view of the bay. I looked at my Italian marble floors and realized they could use a bit of polishing. It had been awhile since I had been here. I walked over to my Sub-Zero and Miele appliances and grabbed a beer from the fridge. It was ice cold, just how I liked it. My kitchen was an open-floor plan with Carrara marble countertops and dark wenge Italian cabinetry.

I started stripping out of my clothes as I walked toward the master bedroom. I thought Charlotte was okay, but there was no place like home. My bathroom features a Jacuzzi that I could not wait to get into. Yes, a nigga loves to soak in the tub. It also had a separate shower and a private balcony. "This could have all been yours, Keena," I said aloud. "But no, you want to play with a nigga's heart and shit." She was about to find out the hard way that I was *not* the one to fuck with.

I picked up the remote that was on the countertop and pushed the button to pull back my custom linen blackout curtains. As I eased into my Jacuzzi, I had Keena on my brain. I cannot believe this bitch played me. I came back to Miami to get my girl back. Fuck Black. He was *not* taking her from me.

My mind drifted off to Ebony. I was grooming her to be my bitch. I sent her to Black to help set him up. That bitch somehow ended up falling in love with him. My brother and I were trying to take the city away from him at the time. After Black killed my brother, it was no longer just about the money. It had become personal. There was no coming back from this. I was going to take all Black's money, along with his life. When he killed my brother Turk, a piece of me died along with him.

I don't know what it is about this nigga that women keep falling for him. When I met Keena, she did not need any grooming. She was already a boss bitch and was robbing niggas. I just had to educate her about Black because she knew nothing about him. Once she researched him, she realized this would be a lick of a lifetime. After learning about him, she knew it would not be easy to get next to him because he had trust issues. He never kept a woman around him long enough to get close to him. She knew after this lick, she could retire, and that's what I was banking on. I wanted her to be *my* woman. We were going to enjoy Black's wealth together.

After what seemed like hours, I finally got out of the tub. I did not want my skin to start shriveling up like a prune, but I had not felt this relaxed in a long time. Stress was a fool, and it was something I did not need.

I reached for a towel, and my Zyprexa fell on the floor. I picked up the bottle and threw it against the wall. I did not give a fuck what those doctors said. I did *not* need that shit. They did not know *anything* about me. How the fuck can they diagnose me with some shit? I had gotten diagnosed right after I killed my aunt. Nobody even knows I killed her. I made it look like an accident, but I drowned that nasty-ass bitch.

She took me in along with my brother after our mom died. She used to make me eat her old, shriveled-up-ass pussy. Man, she was not the cleanest woman. Her pussy used to stank so bad I would always throw up after finishing. But for some reason, she also thought she had the best pussy. She used to say, "I know you enjoy eating this pussy." I just wanted to slap her ass.

One day, she decided to take a bath. I say "decided" because she did not take them often. She called me into the bathroom to wash her. She lay back with her eyes closed. She was so relaxed she did not even see me coming. I forcefully pushed her head down in the water while I watched her try to catch her breath, sucking in water. Then I waited hours before I called the paramedics. I wanted it to look like I was just concerned because she had been in there too long. I put on a good show when the paramedics got there. The police ruled it an accident, and I never looked back. Shortly after that, I got diagnosed with bipolar disorder.

When social services got there after being called by the police because my brother and I were underage, they looked around at our living conditions. Our house was just nasty as hell. Beer bottles lined the stairs, and the kitchen sink was full of dirty dishes. Nasty, blood-stained panties were everywhere. The cleanest part in our house was Turk's and my room, and our bathroom. We came from a clean house, so being nasty was *not* an option. I don't even know how my aunt was kin to my mom because my mom was so clean you could eat off her floors.

I never knew who our dad was. My mom never talked about him. Well, let me say, I was not sure, but I kind of had an idea who he was, although I never had any proof. All I know is the man I thought was my dad is dead and gone now. My brother always swears he used to talk to him, but I was never trying to hear it. I always kept what he said about him in the back of my mind. I could not miss something that was never in my life, but Turk wanted more. That's why he made it his business to find out. Whenever Turk asked my mom about him, she would change the subject like he had not asked her anything. My mom knew who he was; she just did not want him to be a part of our life for whatever her reasons were.

I had heard rumors from other family members that he was the leader of the Blood gang. They say once my mom found out she was pregnant, she wanted more for us, but my dad was not trying to let that life go. The only reason he spared her life was because of us. This was all just rumors, though, because, as I said, my mom never talked about him.

I walked into my bedroom with my phone in my hand. I was trying to call Keena. I had been calling her all fucking night and day. Where the fuck is she? She better not be with that nigga. She's going to make me kill both of them. I don't understand why these females will not let me change. Every time I try to do better, they fuck it up. I do not be wanting to hurt them, but they don't leave me any other choice. I checked her social media pages, but she had no recent posts. That did not mean much, but it doesn't hurt to check.

Keena still was not picking up the phone. I began to text her, praying that she would respond. I know I have sent her over fifty damn text messages. She is not that damn busy that she cannot answer. "Come on, Joc. Get it together," I said to myself.

I walked over to the aquarium that I had built into the wall. It was the only time I had peace. Something about watching the fish swim always calmed me. It was a hundred-gallon fish tank with all types of tropical fish in there. But my favorite one was the electric blue Cichlid. In my sick mind, I knew why it was my favorite fish. That fish was a bully. It was overly aggressive with smaller fish. But on the positive side, I liked the colorful visual it created in the tank.

I decided to try Keena one more time before I went to sleep. I was tired, and the sun was draining me. Just as I expected, she did not pick up her phone. So finally, I drifted off to sleep with her on my mind.

Keena

I was about to power off my phone when I caught Seth looking at me sideways. I could not really blame him with the way my phone was going off. I know he was thinking about the conversation we had earlier about me not closing some "chapters." He probably thought I was still trying to hang on to something, but I was not. I mean, what did Joc want with me? He acted as if we were a couple. He was calling like I owed him some money or something. I knew that was not the case because I served him. He did *not* serve me. On top of the numerous calls, he had sent about fifty damn text messages. If I did not respond to the first ten, what made him think I would respond to the other forty? But we are *not* a couple, so I don't know why he keeps blowing up my line like that. I don't have to respond to his phone calls and text messages just because he says so. Yeah, I did like him at one point, but that's as far as it went. I was never in love with him. Now, I am starting to think I dodged a bullet by not taking it there with him. Something always seemed a little off with him, but I just couldn't put my finger on it . . . yet. I wish I had noticed it earlier.

I thought back to the day I met Joc. Gary, the nigga I usually sold my stolen drugs to, had just gotten in trouble. Gary had told Joc about me because Joc typically bought weight from Gary. I was initially hesitant about the meeting since Gary had gotten busted. I was not sure if he were solid. He could have told the cops anything to save his own ass. I sure did not want to walk into a setup because I did not know Joc. I was not too keen on meeting new people.

At the first meeting, I did not even bring the product. In my mind, if the police did show up, they would have just been showing up for nothing. It would have been an empty bust.

I had pulled up to a house in Grier Heights we had agreed upon as our meeting spot. I later found out that it was Joc's trap house. I pulled up to the trap house on business, like I normally do. I never mixed business with pleasure. Gary made it easy anyway because he was a big, black, ugly dude. He kind of put you in the mind of Deebo from the movie *Friday*, only he was ten times darker than Deebo.

When Joc walked out the door to greet me, my whole mouth fell open. He was too sexy for his own damn good, but now that I think back on it, he did have that little "sneaky" look. That was saying a lot coming from me since I was still a virgin and did not let a man get too close to me. After meeting with him a few times, I realized he was cool, and he started telling me all about this nigga named Black. He told me how much money we could make off Black.

I had been studying Black for a year and knew I would have to move to Miami to get close to him. There was no other way around it. What I did *not* plan on was falling in love with him. Black is a real sweetheart and was everything I wanted and needed in a man. He reminded me so much of my own father that it was scary. In the streets, he was a goon, but nobody knew that soft, sensitive side that I saw. He laid all that street stuff to the side when he was with me. He opened doors for me and cooked for me. He accepted me calling him Peter after I explained my reasons why. When I let him have my most prized possession, my virginity, I knew there was no turning back.

No other man had ever even got a whiff of my pussy. And now, I'm sitting here regretting the last forty-eight hours. I wish I could turn back the hands of time. I don't know what will happen when Peter finally wakes up. I just pray that he believes me and finds it in his heart to forgive me.

I had already told Seth why I had fallen out with Peter. Peter was his best friend. Seth would not hesitate to put a bullet in my head. I am not the average female, but I knew I was not a match for Seth. I did not need the extra stress because this was not looking good.

We were both in Peter's room, along with his mom and sister. The normal crinkle in her face from her beautiful smile turned into worry lines etched across her countenance. His mom looked so lost and hurt. I knew she was probably thinking back to when she lost Peter's dad in the same way. I know this was a mother's worst nightmare having to think about burying her child.

It was hard for me to read her thoughts about me because she had not expressed any words verbally. I could see blood oozing from his sister, Paulina's, fingers as she continuously bit down on her nails. I thought back to the time when she was abducted and kidnapped. Her fingers were raw and tender then. I thought it was something her abductors had done. I realize now I was wrong. It must be a habit she picked up when she was nervous or upset about something.

You could hear a rat piss on cotton, it was so quiet in the room. Finally, I decided to break the silence. "Mrs. Jones and Seth, I'll be back. I'm going to check on Kim." Nobody stopped me as I made a beeline toward the door.

Kim

I was propped up in my hospital bed, flipping through the channels. I can't say if anything was on because I honestly wasn't paying attention. My mind was drifting everywhere. I don't know why I never reached out to Keena when I first realized I was addicted to cocaine. I was so ashamed, and trying to keep my secret made me push my only friend away. Keena was genuinely a nice person. She went hard for the people that she loved. I was one of the people that she loved, and I knew she would go over the top for me. Lately, I have been a bitch to her. I probably have permanently severed our relationship. I pray that I haven't because, as I said, I don't have anybody else.

I thought back to the day I met Keena. I had been in the group home for three days when she moved in. She moved in with a bunch of stuff, and I thought to myself, there is no way this rich, stuck-up girl belongs in here. This has got to be a mistake, and I was waiting for someone to come back and get her. After about a week of her still being there, I realized she was there to stay.

Two weeks went by of us being roommates, and I finally introduced myself to her. I did not talk to anybody else in the group home, and she didn't either. We became fast friends, and here we are now.

Seth is proving to me more and more each day how much he loves me. I am woman enough to admit that I have been through a lot of men. I am not proud of it, but it's the truth. None of them compares to the love that Seth is showing me. Most of the men only used me because they knew I was vulnerable and looking for love. I never really had a man in my life to show me what real love was. My mom told me my daddy was dead as soon as I was old enough to ask about him. My stepfather wasn't shit, so I never really had that father figure.

While thinking about this, the room to my door opened, and in walked Keena. To say her smile lit up the entire room was an understatement. I knew she was happy to see me, but I could also see a hint of sadness on her face. I knew Keena very well. She did not have to tell me something was bothering her. I could sense it.

"Hey, Kim, I'm happy to see that you awoke and are starting to look like yourself."

"Hey, Keena," I greeted her as she bent over to kiss me on my cheek. I moved my legs over so that she could sit on the bed.

"Talk to me, Kim. What's going on?" she asked as I watched the tears form in her eyes.

I began to tell her everything that happened and how Bone tricked me that night. Then after I explained it all to her, I waited for her to ask me the one question I knew was on her mind.

"That lick we pulled on Bone was personal, wasn't it?"

I nodded as I ran my fingers through my nappy weave. I felt even more ashamed because I knew my personal vendetta against Bone could have cost us our lives. Keena was innocent and could have become a fatality due to my selfishness.

"Kim, you could have gotten us killed. That lick was poorly planned, and you didn't think it through at all." Keena then began to tell me what went down with Peter. Just as she was finishing, Seth walked in the door. My nerves started doing all types of flips because I wasn't sure if he had heard anything. He looked back and forth between us like he had something he wanted to say.

"What are you two in here talking about?"

"Nothing," Keena said as she made her way over to the couch so Seth could sit beside me on the bed. He gave me a peck on the cheek. I could not help but smile because I knew my breath was tart. That only gave me confirmation that he loved my dirty drawers. I knew I had to kick this nasty cocaine habit—not only for myself but also for the people that loved me. We sat around and talked for hours until Keena left to go home and get me some things from the condo.

Chapter 27

Joc

I woke up the following day feeling refreshed, but I could feel the heat from the Miami sun beaming through my window. I reached for my phone as I stretched my body out, praying that Keena had called me while I was asleep. When I picked it up, I noticed it was off, which means I forgot to put it on the charger. I didn't want to get up to get my charger, but curiosity killed the cat, so I made my way to the kitchen, where I grabbed some apple juice out of the refrigerator and returned to my room. Once I plugged my phone in, I had to wait a few minutes to power it back on.

When the phone came on, I had no notifications, not even a voicemail indicating that she tried to call me. I debated whether I should send her another text message when something told me to check Facebook. The first post I saw was from an old whore I used to fuck named Tiffany. She swears she was at a loss for words from the shooting of Black. Tiffany will fuck any nigga for money, so I would not be surprised if she had fucked Black. What I *was* surprised at was the fact that someone shot him. My mind was all over the place trying to figure out who could get that close to that nigga. I didn't have to wonder long because all of Miami was talking about this nigga like he was a celebrity or something. They were making my skin crawl with all this disgusting bullshit.

I was reading all the comments, and my eyes got big when one girl commented that she heard a bitch tried to take him out of the game. I ain't even going to lie. A nigga was happy as hell at the thought that Keena probably shot him. That means she did not forget about me. I told myself that was the reason she didn't respond to any of my calls and text messages . . . because she could not. That would make her seem suspect.

I immediately searched on the Miami police inmate website to see if she had been arrested. It dawned on me then that I wasn't even aware if Keena was her real name. I was so focused on trying to get Black that I never really did my homework on her. I was so blinded by trying to wife her that I wasn't even thinking straight. After about twenty minutes of not finding her, I gave up. By then, I was pacing my living room, mad as hell. Keena still was not picking up the phone. Now, it seems like she's sending me straight to voicemail. I need to know what is going on with her. I don't want to have to kill this bitch too.

Seth

I was back home trying to handle some business when I heard a telephone ringing. I barely heard it, but I could hear a rat piss on cotton. That was part of being a street nigga. I often heard the craziest things. I followed the phone's ringing, but it stopped before I reached it. Then suddenly it started ringing again. It was behind the toilet in the hall bathroom. I already knew the phone belonged to Shonte because nobody else had been to my house. The name on her phone said "Ashton." Who the hell is that I wondered. I had never heard that name, and it was a 704 area code. I did not know where that was, but I was about to Google it. Once I typed the area code in Google, Charlotte, North Carolina, popped up. I did not want to accuse her of anything, but I was curious. I saw she had several missed calls from him, so he wanted to talk to her badly. I was not that nigga to be going through her phone, so I walked back to my room to place it on my dresser.

Then I walked into my loft and looked over my house. I stayed in a new development and had not been there long. I bought this house hoping to raise my family in it one day. I hope Shonte is the one I would start my family with. It was crazy how much I was feeling this girl. I was in love with her already. I laughed as I thought about how I was in love with a cokehead. I will not even fuck a cokehead. That shit turns me off, and I don't know how I missed the signs. The only reason I was still entertaining her is because of how she got hooked on that shit. Shonte is my baby, and I'm going to help her kick this nasty-ass habit.

I looked down into my sunken living room, which had floor-to-ceiling mirrors. I loved mirrors. I even had one on the ceiling in my bedroom. I loved to watch Shonte bounce on my dick. The rails on my spiral staircase were a deep dark wood that matched my hardwood floors in the living room. I had a Steinway Model A Salon Grand A piano sitting in the middle of my living room. I low-key liked orchestra music. I could even play the piano. Nobody knew about that, though, not even Black.

I also loved to read, and my three built-in bookshelves proved that. I had all types of books, from self-help even down to Urban. A hot new writer was out named Shmel Carter. I went to the last book fair she had. She has her own book fair every year called the Queen City Book Fair. I bought every paperback she wrote.

Even though my house sat on the water, I still had a built-in underground pool in my backyard and a jacuzzi. Suddenly, I was snapped out of my thoughts by the ringing of my telephone. I looked at my phone and noticed it was Black's mom calling. I suddenly got a bad feeling. I was praying she wasn't calling me with any sad news.

"Hey, Ma, what's up?"

"Do you remember meeting my new neighbor?"

"No, I never got to meet him. I do remember Peter mentioning him to me, though. Why are you asking?"

"Well, he asked me about Peter yesterday. He said he needed to speak with him. I'm not sure what's happening, but maybe you can speak with him since Peter can't."

"I'll get around to speaking to him. Are you still at the hospital?"

"No, I had to leave. I don't like seeing my son like that. I like Keena, do not get me wrong, but something is not adding up with her story. I know Peter loves her, but getting upset about another man just doesn't seem right to me."

"I said the same thing, Ma. I don't want to jump to any conclusions until I speak with Peter, in case she's telling the truth. I know he loves her too and would be mad if something happened to her. I'm on my way back to the hospital now."

"Okay, baby. I'll talk to you later."

I went to my room so I could get ready to head out. I was going to stop somewhere and grab some food for Shonte and me to eat. I knew Keena still was not there because she had sent me a text message saying she was at home about to take a nap. I wonder what this nigga Quan needed to speak with Black about. I only knew his name because Black had mentioned it to me. He was mad as hell because Quan's little brother called himself liking Paulina. Personally, I thought it was funny, but Black was not trying to hear that shit. Well, whatever it was would have to wait.

Keena

As soon as I entered my door, I kicked my shoes off. I was tired as hell, and a shower was way overdue. I also knew I had to call Joc's nagging ass back before he got me killed. I could not understand why he kept damn calling me. This shit was really starting to piss me the fuck off. I purposely powered off my phone so Seth would not get any crazy thoughts.

Finally, I stepped out of the shower, and as soon as I powered on my phone, it started going off. I had five damn text messages from Joc's ass alone. I had a few voicemails which I'm sure came from him. Then I saw a text message from Becky, so I decided to open that one first. She told me that she deposited some money into my account from one of the Laundromats I owned. Money always made me smile. Well, it did make me smile until I met Peter, that is. This man was every damn thing to me. I prayed he pulled through and would forgive me.

Then I went to Joc's messages to see what he wanted. All of them said to call him until I got to the last one, and he said, do not make him kill me. Now, I know this nigga has lost his damn mind if he thinks he's going to do anything to me. He better check my damn record. My damn murder game is on point. I am *not* afraid to pull the damn trigger. All my fear went out the window the day my father got killed. I was about to call him and give him a piece of my mind. I don't play with my life, so he cannot be threatening me.

"Hello," he answered on the first ring like he had the phone in his hand or something.

"Joc, I don't know what your problem is, but don't be sending me no damn threatening text messages. I don't play about my life, and I ain't a scared li'l bitch, and you know that. Now, why the hell are you calling and texting my damn phone?" I was talking so fast, and he tried to interrupt, but I would not let him get a word in until I finished.

"Keena, don't think I don't mean what I said. Bitch, I don't make threats. Anything I motherfucking say is a damn promise, and you can believe that."

I looked at that nigga through the phone because he had me fucked up talking to me all crazy.

"Joc, I don't know when our relationship turned to you disrespecting me, but I haven't done a thing to you. Now, you better pipe the fuck down."

"I'm the one who put you on Black, and now you trying to keep it all to yourself. That was *not* the deal. You got ghost, and I ain't heard nothing from you. And now you tell *me* to pipe the fuck down. No, *you* better pipe the fuck down. Loyalty means a lot to me, and you fucked that up. If you think Black is a ruthless nigga, you ain't seen nothing yet. I will be in Miami to fuck you up since you think I'm playing with your ass."

Then he hung up the phone in my face, but I was not even bothered. As I said, I was not the average female. I will make shit shake. My daddy did *not* raise a damn punk. Since Joc wants to act stupid, I will show his punk ass. If war is what he wants, I will bring it to him. I hate that it had to come to this because I did like him as a friend. I was not trying to keep anything from him. I was ignoring him because I was trying to find a way to tell him I could no longer go through with it. Kim was mad at me at first, but now she understands. She has fallen hard for Seth and does not want to cause him any harm.

I could pack up and move back to Charlotte, but that would be a bitch move. I have never run from anything, and I'm not about to start now. I want to be here when Peter wakes up so I can explain myself. I gave him my virginity, so he should know that I'm in love with him. As far as Joc goes, I am worried, but I ain't. I'm worried because I don't need any more problems right now. I know I'll have to tell Seth about it eventually, and he's going to want to know why this nigga is after me. I don't want Seth looking at me sideways about it just in case things work out with Peter. I'm not worried about Joc because I know I can handle my own. I'm a real boss lady. I'm classy, but I *will* fuck some shit up.

I lay in my bed, and my thoughts drifted to my childhood when my daddy was alive. I smiled, thinking about the many memories we had. My best one was when he took me to the carnival on Freedom Drive. It used to be in the Kmart parking lot every year. There was a big ole teddy bear that I wanted, and my daddy kept trying to win it for me. He spent $300 trying to win that bear. The man finally just gave it to me because he said, technically, my daddy had already bought it a few times. I still have that bear to this day. I reached over and grabbed my teddy bear. It had a little wear and tear on it. Its left eye had a little crack, and the fur was a little thin now, but the bear was my comfort when I was in my feelings. Right now, I was in my feelings with everything going on.

Chapter 28

Quan

I sat and stared at the picture on my phone. I had my homegirl from Charlotte send me a picture she had taken at the Epic Center last year. I knew that girl my neighbor's son had with him looked awfully familiar. She was sitting there lying, talking about she's from Atlanta. That bitch is from Charlotte. Well, she may be from Atlanta, but she damn sure lives in Charlotte. I wonder why she told a bald-faced lie like that. The one thing I cannot stand is a liar.

I sent my homegirl a text message and asked her what the girl's name was and how she knew her. When she told me they grew up in a group home together, I knew then that she had some shit with her. I don't really know that nigga Peter, but I knew what he did. His mom might have been blind to the fact, but nothing was slow about me. I was trying to be down with his team. With the weight that nigga be pushing, I can go back to Charlotte and be the kingpin. I knew this information would prove my loyalty, so I told his mom I needed to talk to him.

Today, she told me he would not be able to talk to me for a while, but his best friend would. That was fine with me. I knew, either way, I would win some brownie points with this information. So, no, I did not feel like a bitch-ass nigga. I gotta take care of my mom and little brother, so fuck everybody else.

Seth

On my drive to the hospital, so many thoughts were swimming in my head. It's funny that I'm a drug dealer, but I hate the existence of drugs. My sister was strung out badly, and it hurts my heart to watch how drugs destroyed her life. My nephew was her world at one point in her life, but now, drugs mean more to her than her son. I know it's putting a toll on my mom. Physically, I can't do much because I be in the streets too much. Financially, I make sure both are straight. That's why I moved them out of Miami. I wanted my nephew to have a better upbringing. I bought my mom a house in Chester, South Carolina. She loves it there.

I saw all the signs with my sister, but somehow, I missed them with Shonte. I'm not sure how that happened. I love that girl with everything in me. I'm mad at myself for missing them. Now that I think back, *all* the signs were there before my eyes. I just didn't want to believe that a female I was in love with could be a cokehead. I have never had a girlfriend before. I have had a few girls that I have smashed, but they didn't mean shit to me. I wasn't looking for nothing with Shonte, but it happened. I thought I could just fuck her too like I did all the other females, but there was something about her that made me fall for her. She was different. She listened to me, and she always looked past my hood shit. She knew there was more to me than the streets. What I loved the most about her was she had her own. She never asked me for shit.

I never really knew what she did for a living. I hate to admit it, but it was the truth. She told me she had a trust fund that she was living off from when her mom died. I mean, I had no other choice but to believe her. She didn't give me any reasons to doubt her. My gut feeling was telling me there was more to her story, though, and I plan on finding out. When she gets out of that hospital, she has a lot of explaining to do, including this nigga Ashton that keeps calling her damn phone. One thing I knew was that I was for real about us, and I didn't want any secrets between us. I was all in, and I needed her to be as well. I turned the corner—and instantly, my thoughts were interrupted.

Boom! Boom! Boom!

I heard the gunshots as I drove down Douglas Road, and I knew that whoever it was, *I* was their target. I swerved, almost hitting the fire hydrant on the street corner. Somebody was bold as hell coming for me. I looked in front of me and saw a yellow Charger speeding down Main Highway, so I took off after the car like a bat out of hell. He was speeding. I now had a vision of him, but I didn't know this nigga. I was trying to figure out what the beef was he had with me.

He turned down Royal Road so fast I could hear the tires screeching, and I was hot on his ass. I pulled out my .47 Magnum and shot at his car. He swerved, but he was not fast enough. The bullet went through his trunk. That didn't stop that nigga, though. He kept right on driving. When he turned on Franklin Avenue, he got away, and I was mad as hell. I was angry, but I had his license plate in my mental Rolodex. I knew I would catch up to that nigga because I had a homegirl that worked for the DMV, and I quickly dialed her number. I was so damn mad I didn't know what to do with myself.

"Hello," I heard her sweet voice through my car speakers. She sounded like that singer Michel'le over the phone. Her voice aggravates the shit out of me, but she's a sweet girl. She had poor taste in men, though, and I told her every chance I got. I couldn't stand her bitch-ass nigga, and it wasn't on no jealous type of shit either. I just hated how he was running around Miami, making her look stupid. I always see that nigga in the strip club, and he be fucking they nasty ass too. In my opinion, she could do better. She's a pretty girl, and she got her shit together, but I stopped telling her about that no-good nigga because she always got mad at me like *I* was the one cheating on her. I didn't understand women sometimes, but she was my friend for real. She was the female version of Black. We all grew up together on the playground, but those two were not as close as she and I were. Black just kind of distanced himself over the years. No love is lost, and she knows Black wouldn't hesitate to put a bullet in a nigga, if necessary.

"What's up, Michel'le?" I was already laughing when she picked up the phone. She was laughing at my joke as well because I always called her that. But even though I was making jokes, there wasn't a damn thing funny at this moment. "Somebody just tried to kill my ass," I was yelling at her through the phone.

"What? Slow down, Seth. What are you talking about, and why are you yelling at me? You better calm down. You know better than to talk to me like that." Sarita could always check me, and I wouldn't say anything back to her. She was right. I was out of character yelling at her, but I was upset. Quickly I calmed down and began to tell her everything that had happened, even down to Black getting shot.

"You mean to tell me Black got shot by a bitch? I had heard the rumor but didn't think it was true. I was going to call you today anyway so I can go see him."

"Yes, he did get shot by a female. But I don't want to disrespect her until I find out what happened. We both know that when that nigga loves, he loves hard and don't play that disrespect shit."

"Yes, I do have to agree with you on that, but back to somebody trying to kill you . . . What are you talking about?" I began to explain to her what had just happened, then she told me she was off work for the next two days, but she would handle it once she got back.

"You don't have a coworker you can ask? I ain't trying to wait no two days. This motherfucker just tried to kill me. I need to get on his ass."

"Do you *really* want me to ask a coworker? When that nigga come up dead, she will remember looking his ass up, and I don't want that shit tied back to me. I been knowing you all my life. That nigga should have killed you because he just signed his own death certificate. You're going to kill him."

I thought about what she said, and she was right. And I didn't want anything tying back to her because I *will* kill that nigga. "You know what? You're right, Sarita. Clearly, I was not thinking. My mind is all over the place. This nigga, whoever he is, got me fucked up."

"I know you're mad, but you need to think rationally. This is not the Seth that I know because the Seth that I know would haven't said none of the shit you just said."

"Okay, Sarita. You need to go see Black too. I don't want to hear you were 'planning' on it. You already know you don't have to call me to see him. All of us are friends. I don't know what happened between y'all that you grew apart, but we all are friends. So get up there and see him. I'm on my way up there now."

"I am going to see him. I'll get by there soon."

We hung up, and I headed to the hospital.

Sarita

I know Seth thinks that me and Black just grew apart, but it ain't like that. Black and I have some history that Seth don't know anything about. I thought back to the real reason why we grew apart. It was the summer right before our senior year, and I was hanging out with both like I usually did. Seth had gotten a phone call from one of his thots of the week, and he decided to bounce to go see what was up with her. My parents were at work, so it was just Black and I. Black used to be shy in school, so I'm shocked that he is the way he is now. I guess losing his dad, and then Ebony, did something to him. I was a virgin, and so was he. Seth was the only one getting it on a regular, and he assumed Black was too. I was the only one that knew Black was a virgin. He always told me it was no big deal, and when the time was right, he would lose his virginity with the right female. I guess he thought I was that female. That night, we lost our virginity to each other.

"What's up, Sarita?" Black had said as he leaned in to kiss me on my lips. His lips were so soft for a boy. They felt like cotton. I started kissing him back when I felt him tugging on my shorts. I was hesitant initially, but I eased up and let him have his way. The next thing I knew, we were on my bed, and Black was between my legs. Even at 17, he was working with a monster, and at that time, he didn't know what to do with it. I know he's probably an expert now. I was scared, but I didn't want him to know just how frightened I was. I had my eyes closed and had been holding my breath and didn't even realize it until he told me to breathe. When I looked into Black's eyes, I knew he was just as scared as I was.

I felt the head of his dick trying to enter my pussy, and I tensed up. "Relax," he whispered in my ear. I let my guard down as he slowly entered me with no protection. Since we both were virgins, we knew there was no way to catch anything. Getting pregnant was the last thing on both our minds, so imagine my surprise when my period didn't show up for two months. I didn't think anything of it at first. I just blamed it on being stressed out. My parents were going through a divorce, and my grandma had just died. But reality set in when the morning sickness kicked in. I knew my worst nightmare had become a reality, and I was scared.

I went to Black first because I wanted to see where his head was at. To my surprise, he wanted the baby. But I had my whole life ahead of me and couldn't see myself being a mother right now. I had big dreams and ambitions. I was going to college. I have wanted to attend Florida A&M since I was a little girl. My mom used to take me to watch the band perform because she was alumni. I wanted to be a Fam U Diamond, which is the name of the band's dance girls. I danced all through high school with our marching band. Tryouts were in March, and I would have been good and pregnant by that time. Black knew how important that was to me. It was all I talked about.

When I told my mom I was pregnant, she didn't hesitate to take me to get an abortion. I got the abortion behind Black's back, and he was furious when he found out. He told me then that he would never look at me the same again. I still have regrets about it to this day, but there is nothing I can do about it now.

I was attending Florida A&M at the same time as his girlfriend Ebony. I didn't like that bitch. I knew Black used to flaunt her around campus, trying to hurt me, and it did. I was hurt beyond measure. I knew I would probably still be with Black to this day if I hadn't killed our baby, but I had to do what was best for me.

The night Ebony got killed, I watched how the scene played out once Black got there. I wanted to reach out and hug him, but I was at a loss for words. I didn't know what to say. I didn't like the girl, but I didn't wish death on her. Not liking her had nothing to do with Black, though. There was just something about her sneaky ass. I tried to tell Black she was sneaky, but he told me to mind my own business. I was taken aback by that. I know I hurt him, but I at least thought we could remain friends. After that, he told me he would always be there for me if I needed him, but our friendship was over. That hurt me more than anything because we were friends first. If I knew having an abortion would ruin our friendship, I would have pushed rewind on the tape, and we would have never had sex.

I tried to reach out to him again after Ebony's funeral, but he pushed me away again. He said the most hurtful thing to me that day, and I never let it go. He looked me in my eyes and said I was probably happy that she was dead. I asked him how he could fix his mouth to say that, and he said I like "killing people" and walked off, leaving me looking stupid.

I can pretty much say whatever relationship we had left was over after that. I did know that if I needed him, he would be there as promised, but I never called on him for anything. Now, he was lying in the hospital, fighting for his life. I knew I needed to put my pride to the side and check on him. We had been friends for too long, and I would be hurt if something happened to him. With that thought, I busted a U-turn in the middle of the street and headed to the hospital.

Black

I don't know what is going on. I hear people talking all around me, but they can't hear me. I keep trying to speak, but it's like I am being ignored. I heard Keena crying, and I was trying to figure out what all the fuss was about. My dad even came and talked to me last night. He has never come back and talked to me as long as he has been dead. He told me to forgive Keena because she was the woman for me, but I don't even know what she did that I need to forgive her for. I vaguely remember what I am even here for.

I heard somebody come into my room. I tried to open my eyes to see who it was. I kept hearing him saying, "Mr. Jones, blink if you hear me." I'm assuming it was the doctor. It was like I was willing myself to open my eyes . . . but I couldn't. He walked toward my bed, and I could see the light coming from his flashlight as he forcefully opened my eyes. I started slightly moving my head from side to side to indicate that I was awake and could hear him. At first, he didn't notice it until a female said, "Dr. Von, there is movement."

The doctor pushed my call bell and started yelling out orders. The next thing I knew, many people flooded my room. Someone was taking blood, and someone else ran a pencil over my feet. So much chaos was going on that I felt like I was part of a circus. The best part came when someone began removing the tubes down my throat.

After all the commotion died down in my room, Seth busted through the door. I could tell by the scowl on his face that something was wrong with him. He was so upset about whatever was happening with him that he didn't even notice I was awake, and the tubes were gone. He flopped down on the couch in my room and started going through his phone, still not paying any attention to me. Shortly after that, Sarita walked through the door. Now, *that* was a total surprise because I hadn't seen her since Ebony's funeral. I knew Seth still talked to her, and I never told him what went down between her and me. I don't know what he thinks happened. Even though what she did hurt me, I still didn't have it in me to make her look bad.

"What's up, Sarita?"

Finally, Seth looked up with a shocked expression on his face.

"Oh shit, Black. When did you wake up?" I muffled out a forced laugh. It was forced because it hurt too much to laugh.

"Nigga, I have watched you play on your phone for ten minutes, and you didn't look at me one damn time. What the hell is wrong with you anyway? I saw you walk in here with a scowl on your ugly-ass face."

"Man, fuck you," he said as he walked over to the bed and embraced me in a brotherly hug. "I am *so* happy to have my brother back. Man, don't you ever scare me like that again."

I looked up at Sarita and noticed she would not even look at me. Then I looked at Seth to see if he noticed it too, but he wasn't paying either of us any attention. He was all in his phone.

He finally finished messing with his phone and acknowledged my question. He began to tell me what had happened to him on his way to see me. "Enough about me, though, nigga. What the fuck happened between you and Keena?"

"What you mean, what happened? Where is Keena anyway? Why isn't she here?"

"She's been here, but she went home to shower and get some rest. She'll probably be back soon."

I lay there and listened to Seth tell me about how I ended up in the hospital. I didn't remember any of what he was telling me. I didn't know what to believe. I mean, Keena was wifey, so I know she wouldn't hurt me on purpose. I knew it had to be an accident. I was mad because I couldn't remember anything about what had happened to land me here.

At the mention of Keena's name, I noticed the mean mug that Sarita had on her face. I was trying to figure out what *that* was all about. She knew she fucked up with me when she told me she killed my child. I mean, I still got love for her. How could I not? I've known her my whole life. She had no reason now to be all in her feelings because she knew we could never be together again. The truth is I *did* care for her. I always have. I'd wanted her to be my girlfriend since the sandbox. I knew I wanted to lose my virginity to her. But I didn't want no shit when Keena came here, meaning I didn't want those crazy-ass looks Sarita was giving. I don't like a bunch of drama, which is why I was not the player type. It brought too much attention. One female was enough for me.

Chapter 29

Keena

I walked into Peter's hospital room, and my jaw dropped. I looked over at Seth and stuck my middle finger up because he could have told me Peter had woken up. To say I was shocked was an understatement. I wanted to be prepared just in case Peter was mad because I did not want to walk into an ambush.

"Why are you standing over there?" Peter asked me with his arms stretched out for a hug. I embraced him and gave him a wet kiss with tears running down my face. I didn't know what to expect, but I was sure glad he was not upset with me. I soon found out why he wasn't upset when he spoke up.

"I hate this shit. I cannot even remember how I ended up in the hospital, but Seth says you shot me. I know you would not do it on purpose, so what happened? I mean, my wife wouldn't do nothing like that."

I swallowed the huge lump in my throat. I was at a loss for words. I did not know what to tell this man. I was happy that he did not remember, but I did not want to lie to him, so I said the first thing that came to mind.

"Baby, we can talk about this another time. You just came out of a coma. Did anybody call your mom?"

"Yes, I sent her a text message," Seth said as he got off the couch.

That was the first time I noticed the girl sitting beside him. I wondered who this chick was and who she was there to see. It couldn't be good if she were there for Seth since he claimed he had love for Kim. Well, I did not have to wonder long because Seth made it his business to introduce us. I noticed her facial expression when he told her I was Peter's girlfriend. There seemed to be more to it than what they were letting on, but I was not going to worry about it. I had to trust my man.

"Well, Black, I'll go ahead and get out of here. I'm happy to see that you're doing better." She then turned to speak to me. "It was nice meeting you, Keona."

"It's Keena, not Keona."

"Whatever," she said as she threw her hands in the air and walked out the door.

See, that right there is why I do not hang around hating-ass hoes, I thought to myself. This girl did not even know me, and she was throwing shade, but for what, I have no idea. I turned and looked at Peter, but he wasn't paying attention to either of us. He was in his own zone. Only God knows what he was thinking about. I was just praying he wasn't getting an instant memory.

"I'm going to let you two talk while I check on Shonte." Seth headed for the door but was stopped in his tracks once Peter started talking.

"What's going on with her?"

"Oh, man, my fault. I was so caught up with what I was telling you happened to me that I forgot to tell you about what happened to her. I'll let Keena tell you. You two need to talk anyway." He walked out the door without even waiting on a response.

I began to tell Peter about what was going on with Kim. I made him remember when I found the powder residue in her room. He stated that he remembered that. We also talked about me shooting him. I told him *almost* everything. I left out certain parts of the story. I did not want to incriminate myself, and I did not want to be on Seth's hit list—not that I was scared, but I knew how to pick and choose my battles. I knew it was only a matter of time before his full memory resurfaced. But I didn't want to think about that right now. I just wanted to enjoy my man by myself until his mom came.

Joc

Keena must think I'm playing with her motherfucking ass. My adrenaline was at an all-time high from the gunfight I had with Seth's bitch ass. I don't know how I missed that nigga. I now had to be on my shit because I already knew how he was coming. I know I said he was a bitch, but that's only a figure of speech. Seth wouldn't hesitate to pull the trigger.

I was now in my room, pacing the floor with sweat dripping down my body. I was going to kill Black and everything attached to his ass. He killed my father, brother, nephew, and just took my girl. I didn't care about Ebony like I did for Keena, so I wasn't thinking about *that* bitch. She wasn't shit anyway. I wonder how that nigga will feel after I reveal to him who Ebony *really* was. I knew that would crush that nigga because he was in love with that bitch.

I just stared at my phone. I couldn't believe Keena tried to play me like that. This bitch obviously didn't know who the fuck I was. That bitch talking about she ain't scared. Hell, she *better* be if she knew what she had coming to her. She only saw the nice side of me. She just didn't know the monster that she had brought back out. I was trying to change, but I swear a ho was going to be a ho. I wanted to call that bitch so bad, but I was going to chill. I knew she would think shit was all sweet if she didn't hear from me. I was going to make a sneak attack on that ass.

Suddenly, I was startled by the ringing phone in my hand. I was so caught up in my thoughts that I didn't realize the phone had been ringing. I looked at the caller ID and realized it was one of my corner boys.

"Nigga, you back in Miami?"

"Why?"

"Man, that nigga Seth just rode through the hood asking about a yellow Charger. I already knew it had to be your ass once he finished describing it."

"What did you tell him?"

"I didn't tell that nigga shit. My loyalty's to you, dawg. He doesn't know who you are, but he got a bounty on your head, my nigga."

"Word? How much is the bounty?"

"That nigga said one hundred thousand for any information leading to the nigga that owns that car. You know it's only a matter of time before somebody rats you out. That nigga's offering too much money."

"What I'm trying to figure out is how did y'all let that nigga walk away alive?"

"That would have been suicide, my nigga. He was rolling deep as hell. Wasn't nobody out here but me and Tim. We were outnumbered."

"Oh, okay, I see. Well, I ain't worried about that nigga. If you catch him sleeping, take his whole damn head off his body and place it on the front porch of Black's mama. I want blood, and I ain't stopping until I make that nigga suffer. I ain't even going to kill Black, but I *am* going to kill everything attached to him. I want that nigga to feel all the pain I been feeling for years."

"Well, I'll let the crew know to be on the lookout, but you already know it's not going to be easy to take him out. That nigga stays ready."

I hung up the phone, mad as hell. I couldn't believe this nigga had the nerve to be coming to *my* hood. I wish somebody would sell me out for some money. I would kill they ass once I found out who it was. I knew I had to take this nigga out soon before he figured out who I was. He did not know me personally, so I knew he would wonder why I was coming for him.

I waited for the night to fall before I decided to hit the streets. I hopped in my all-black Range Rover and sped through the city. I was on a mission. I had one thing on my mind . . . and that was murder. I was going to kill Black's sister and his mom. I was going to make that nigga get up out of that hospital bed and come find me.

I drove to the hospital where Black was, hoping I could catch his mom leaving so I could follow her home. I might even luck up and catch Keena's ho ass. I pulled into the visitors' parking lot and cut my lights. I was going to wait this out.

The next morning, the sun was shining bright on my dashboard. I looked around because I was trying to recognize where I was. Then it became clear to me that I was at the hospital. I must have fallen asleep waiting on Black's mom. I was now mad at myself because I didn't get anything accomplished. But that's okay. I'll catch her ass soon, I said to myself as I pulled out of the parking lot to head home.

My condo was hot as hell when I walked through the door. I went to the thermostat to adjust the air, but it still wouldn't do anything. I immediately dialed the building maintenance man and told him to get his ass up here as soon as possible. I know he heard the base in my voice because he was ringing my doorbell within minutes.

When I opened the door, I couldn't do anything but laugh at his Pee-wee Herman-looking ass. He even had the bow tie and all. I guess he didn't see anything funny because he didn't even smile.

"Yo, nigga. Just fix my shit. I don't have time for all the shenanigans."

"Yes, sir."

I really didn't have a reason to be mad at him. He hadn't done anything to me. I was just frustrated with everything that was going on.

He preceded to do whatever he had to do, and I walked to my room, not thinking any more about his ass. All I had on my mind was this situation at hand with Seth. After all, how the fuck is he even in *my* hood looking for any damn body? Granted, he don't know who it was, but it's not his territory. The maintenance man interrupted my thoughts.

"Sir, I recharged your air conditioner. You should be fine now."

"A'ight, thank you."

"You're welcome." Then he walked back out the door just as quickly as he came. I now had an even better plan than what I originally was thinking. Seth thinks his family is invincible. He got his mom tucked away down in South Carolina like she's untouchable. I'm about to show him she *can* be touched. I'm telling the truth when I say I know everything about these niggas. I been watching them for an exceptionally long time. Seth drives down to Chester, South Carolina, at least once a month and spends three or four days with his mom and nephew. His sister is a dopehead and abandoned her son. She's on that powder bad, and she be popping mollies. I knew her back in the day. She was bad as hell. Her body was banging in all the right places. She had all the niggas checking for her in high school. I don't know much else about his sister other than that because she is hard to keep up with. I *do* know she's still in Miami, but that is the most I can say.

Seth

"What's up with you?" I patted Shonte's leg so she could scoot over on the bed and I could sit down.

"Nothing much. I'm ready to get out of here, and I'm tired of these people poking at me every few hours."

"You'll be out of here soon. I had Keena check out some inpatient rehabs for you. Don't worry about the cost. I'll pay for everything. I love you, Shonte, and I will see you through this. We are in this together," I told her as I reached over and kissed her.

"Thank you," she said with tears in her eyes. I reached my hand up to wipe the tears from her face.

"What are you crying for? I never want to see you drop another tear unless it's a happy one."

"These *are* happy tears, baby. I love you too. No man has ever made me feel this special. I keep pinching myself, waiting to wake up from this wonderful dream."

"Baby, I promise you, this is real. I have never felt like this about a woman before. But if you hurt me, I *will* kill you." I laughed, but I looked her in the eyes at the same time, letting her know I was dead serious. Then I reached into my pocket and pulled out her cell phone. "Some nigga named Ashton keeps blowing up your phone. You better tell that nigga you already got a man," I told her as I placed the phone beside her on the bed.

She looked me in my eyes as she cupped my chin. "You don't have anything to worry about. I met him right before I moved here at Walmart. I talked to him a few times since I been here, but that's it. I am not sure why he keeps calling, as you say, but I promise you there ain't nothing between us."

She just doesn't know that her keeping it real with a nigga made me respect her even more.

I sat and watched a few shows with Shonte and had a few conversations. She told me she would prefer if I called her Kim and not Shonte. She told me her name was Shonte because she didn't think we would go this far. Shonte is her middle name, but she didn't want any secrets between us, either.

"Take me to see Black. I am *not* bedridden. Dang, you act like I'm fragile or something."

"I didn't know you wanted to see him, but I can make that happen." I reached over her and pushed the nurse button so she could bring me a wheelchair.

"Hello, nurse's station."

When the nurse arrived, I said, "I need a wheelchair."

"No, he doesn't."

I looked at her. "Why don't you need a wheelchair? I thought you said you wanted to go see Black."

"I do, but I can walk. I don't need a wheelchair. There's nothing wrong with my legs."

"So, do y'all want the wheelchair or not?"

I had forgotten that the nurse was still there. "Nah, we good. My lady is stubborn." Shonte, I mean Kim, playfully punched me in my arm. "Come on, girl." I helped her out of bed. Then we held hands as we walked toward Black's room. Keena was still in there when we walked in, and she was giving Black a sponge bath.

"Oh Lawd, I didn't want to walk in on this."

"Hush, Seth," Keena said as she flicked water on me. "Hey, Kim," she said as she stopped what she was doing and walked toward her girl to hug her. Kim had her hands stretched out to receive the love.

"Hey, boo. I see you're busy with your man. We'll come back later."

We walked back toward Kim's room as quickly as we left it.

Keena

I left the hospital and headed to Yardbird's because Peter wanted some chicken and waffles. Hands down, they had some of the best fried chicken this side of Florida. Personally, I wanted some shrimp and grits. I had been hungering for it for a few days now. When I walked into the restaurant, some loudmouthed-ass girl was standing at the counter popping gum. She was on her phone talking to somebody, and I honestly didn't think she was paying any attention to me. She was ghetto as fuck, and apparently, I laughed out loud without realizing it. She turned around so quickly with her big, thick-ass braids looking like Craig's girlfriend from *Friday*.

"What the fuck are you laughing at, ho?"

Hearing that, I laughed even harder. This girl was hilarious to me for some reason. Well, that made the situation even worse. She now had her hands on her hips as she rolled her neck around and wagged her finger in the air. The next thing I know, this ho was walking toward me like she wanted to manhandle me.

"You may want to back the fuck up for real because you definitely don't want no smoke." All I knew was that if this bitch got any closer to me, I was going to beat her ass. I didn't come in here for this, and I didn't mean any harm.

"What the fuck is so funny, Keena?"

"Whoa. How the fuck do you know my name?" The look on her face was priceless. I know she slipped when she said my name, but it was too late.

"I don't know your name."

"Bitch, you just said my motherfucking name. Now, I'm going to ask you one more damn time. How the fuck do you know my name?" By this time, the restaurant had gotten quiet. All eyes were on us, but at this point, I didn't give a fuck. I did not know many people in Miami, and of the few people that I did know, this bitch for damn sure was not one of them.

Before I knew it, this bitch had swung on me and hit me. I stumbled back because she had caught me off guard, and I had to catch myself. I felt my eye swelling up. I'm light-skinned, so I knew I would have a shiner. But I came back with a two-piece. I popped that bitch back in her eye. The next thing I knew, we were in a full-fledged catfight. She grabbed my hair, thinking it was a weave and would come out. If I *did* have a weave, she best believe it would be the good shit. But her hand slipped right through my hair because she had nothing to grip. Then I grabbed her by her big ghetto-ass braid and rammed her head into the countertop.

I saw all the cell phones up in the air, so I knew they were taking videos. I didn't want to be on anybody's Facebook acting all crazy because I was too classy for this shit. Next, I reached to my side and pulled out my pistol. I struck her across her face that I heard the bones in her cheek crack. I will teach this bitch about fucking with me.

Suddenly, I heard sirens from a distance, and I knew they were coming for us. I don't know who called the police, but I was not about to stick around and find out. I ran and hopped into my car, mad as hell.

When I got to the stoplight on Lenox Avenue and Fifteenth Street, heading back to the hospital, I finally got a chance to check my eye. That bitch really fucked it up. Not only did I *not* get our food, but also now my eye was fucked up too. I had to explain some unknown shit to Peter. The reason I say it's unknown is that I don't even know this damn girl. For the life of me, I'm trying to figure out how the hell she knows me. After all, that bitch said my name clear as day. On top of that, I had a headache from hell. My head was hurting so bad it was throbbing.

As soon as I walked into Peter's room, I noticed his mom was there, and it seemed as if all eyes were on me.

"What the fuck happened to your eye? Excuse me, Ma. I didn't mean to disrespect you like that. But what happened to your eye, and where's my food?"

"It's a long story, and I don't even know the answers to it."

"Well, I ain't going nowhere anytime soon," he said as he made a hand gesture around the room, indicating that he was in the hospital, like I didn't already know that.

"Peter, can we talk about this later? After all, your mom is here to visit you."

"I feel the same way Peter feels. I want to know what happened to your eye too."

I began to explain to them what went down at Yardbird's. I was still in shock myself because this whole scene was crazy.

"So, let me get this straight. You didn't even know this girl, but she knew you?"

"Yes, Peter, she knew me because she called my name. I think I was more shocked by that than anything else. Everybody I know in Miami is in this hospital, minus your sister, of course. The crazy part is when I called her out on it, she tried to deny it and said she never said my name. The next thing I knew, she punched me in my eye, and all hell broke loose."

"I don't like this at all. Let me call Seth so that he can put his ear to the street. First, somebody shoots at him out of the blue, and now this. This is getting out of hand."

"What do you mean somebody shot at Seth?" my mom asked.

I think Peter realized then he had just said too much in front of his mom. She didn't know anything about this side of Peter. She never knew her son had a dark side. For all she knew, her son was a successful businessman.

"Nothing, Ma. Just some random shooting. Seth just happened to be in the wrong place at the wrong time."

"Oh," she said, placing her hand over her heart like she couldn't bear the news.

I saw Peter pick up his cell phone. I knew he had sent Seth a text message because he didn't want to say much more in front of his mom. This is precisely why I didn't want to say anything either, but he insisted I tell him what happened. I know his mom would have been worried about me, so I had to tell her something. I told them I would be right back and that I had to let Kim know what was going on with me. I knew by now that the news had gotten to Seth, and he had repeated it to Kim.

My suspicion was correct when I walked into her room.

"Oh my God, Keena. Who did this to you? We are going to get that bitch. Just wait until I get out of here."

I couldn't help but laugh. I knew then that my girl was back. Kim has *always* had my back.

"Calm down, Kim. First, I don't even know the girl, so I don't know who to get. Second, you should see that bitch. You *know* I fucked her over. I hit her with my pistol. You know how I come. I wasn't playing no damn games with that bitch."

"Oh, I already know how you come. Damn, I hate that I missed that shit."

"I'm just trying to figure out how and where that bitch knows me from."

"What do you mean, 'know' you?"

"I thought Peter told y'all."

"All he said was you got into a fight, and I told Kim," Seth said.

I explained my story for the second time that day. Seth said he would get on it because this shit sounded suspect as hell to him too. All I know is I agreed with them both. Something strange and mysterious was going on, but I knew Seth would get to the bottom of it without a shadow of a doubt. This bitch had me all the way fucked up.

Joc

I spotted Keena when she first turned into the parking lot of Yardbird, so I immediately hit this ole ghetto-ass chickenhead that I used to fuck named Sheena on her phone. I saw her ass in there too when Keena walked in. I had to promise her a band and some good dick for her to carry it out. What I was *not* expecting was for Sheena to get her ass beat. She used to beat everybody's ass in Liberty Square Apartments. For Keena to beat her ass, I knew she was the damn truth. Nobody—I mean *nobody*—could beat Sheena's ass, and for that, I was mad as hell. I hope she didn't think she was getting paid. However, when my phone started ringing, I knew she did.

"What, bitch?" I answered the phone with an attitude.

"Don't be talking to me like that. I want my motherfucking money."

"Bitch, I ain't giving you shit. You got your ass beat."

"I don't care about nothing you're talking about. I did what you told me to do. I want my motherfucking money, Joc. Not to mention that bitch hit me with her gun."

"As I said, you ain't getting shit. I told you I would pay you to beat *her* ass, and you *didn't. That's* the reason right there that I'm not paying you. Listen, bitch, don't call my phone anymore." I hung up on her. Then a text message came through from Sheena. I laughed at the message she sent, talking about can she still have some dick. This girl was crazy. I just shook my head at her crazy ass. Now, I had to come another way for Keena. I didn't want to kill her, but I wanted to fuck her over. I was still in shock that she whipped Sheena's ass. I knew I would have to send more than one girl at her.

I lay across my bed and scrolled Facebook to see if Keena had posted anything. I typed her name in, and when her page came up, I saw that she had unfriended me. A light laugh escaped my lips. This bitch was doing the most. She better get ready because I am about to wreak havoc in her life—and everybody attached to her.

Chapter 30

Kim

A month later . . .

I walked out of the Adaptive Center, a drug rehab that Seth had enrolled me in, feeling like a new woman. The sun was beaming down on me, and I embraced it all. I had not been on this side of the center since Seth dropped me off a month ago. I heard a horn blow, and Seth was sitting behind the wheel of a candy-apple-red drop-top Mercedes-Benz. It was a C-Class, but that car was so pretty. It was the car I always wanted. Seth hopped out of it as I was walking toward it.

"Don't you want to drive your new car?"

"Shut up, Seth. Are you *serious?* Is this *really* my car?"

"Yes, this is your car. I wouldn't play about something like this."

I started jumping up and down, screaming in joy. The staff in the rehab rushed out of the building to see what was happening. At this point, I did not care what anybody thought. I was too damn happy. I grabbed hold of Seth's face and started kissing him all over. I have never received this much love from a man. I could not believe Seth had bought me a car—and not just *any* car. He bought me a damn Mercedes.

"Baby, what made you buy me a car?"

"Baby, you deserve a car. I know you're tired of riding with Keena's ass."

"A Mercedes, though? You went and bought me a Mercedes, Seth? You say it like you bought me a little ole Honda or something."

"Hey, we can take it back and get you a Honda if it'll make you feel better."

I playfully punched him while I ran to the driver's side and hopped into the seat. I looked around my car before I pulled off. It had soft leather seats the color of peanut butter. I started messing with all the buttons on the dashboard and noticed I had a backup camera. Damn, this car was *everything*. He handed me my phone before I pulled off. I wasn't allowed to have my phone while in rehab, so Seth held it.

"Oh, by the way, that nigga Ashton is going to make me kick his ass."

"Why, bae?"

"He refuses to stop calling your phone even after I told him not to. Hell, I don't understand these niggas. I told him he better go and read that book, *Side Nigga,* by Shmel Carter, and leave mine alone." He was laughing as he said all this.

"What, bae? What's the name of the book? You are such a mess. You'll say anything."

"Nah, I'm for real. It's a book named that. Go on Amazon and look it up."

"I believe you, but I wonder why Ashton keeps calling my phone. This is odd, but anyway, enough about that. Where are Keena and Black? I want to see them. I missed them."

"We're about to head over there now. Trust me, Keena misses you as much as you miss her."

I started laughing.

"What's so funny?"

"You."

"Why? What did I do?"

"You said Keena missed me, so I guess Black ain't thinking about my ass," I playfully said. He realized what he said and started laughing too.

"Girl, you already know I didn't mean it like that. You're a trip."

We pulled up in front of Black's house, and Keena was already outside waiting on me. She ran to my side of the car once I got out.

"This you, bitch?"

"Yes, somebody do love me, or I am throwing that pussy on him right now." We both shared a laugh.

"How about both?" Seth said as he hugged me from behind and kissed me on my neck. I was all smiles at just the touch of him.

We all walked into the house. I looked around Black's place in astonishment. Seth had a nice house, but this was a minimansion. This was my first time in his home.

"It's nice, ain't it?" Keena whispered in my ear as we walked to the theater room. A huge seventy-five-inch plasma television was mounted on the wall. Speakers were all around the room, giving it that movie feel. The chairs were even set up movie-style. Three rows of recliner seats stood there, and you had to climb stairs for each row. His setup was nice.

Black walked into the room and asked if we wanted to cook on the grill. I was down because I had no real food in about a month. The food at the rehab was bland, and whoever the cook was needed to learn the meaning of seasoning salt. "I don't know what you're so hyped about, Kim," Black said as he handed Keena his bank card.

"What do you mean? Shit, I'm hyped because a sister is hungry. They did not feed us nothing in that place. I felt like I was in jail."

"Have you ever been to jail?" Black asked me.

"No."

"Well, how do you know what jail feels like?"

I could not even answer his question because I was only going off what I saw on television.

"I don't know what it feels like, but I *do* know that it was not a pleasant stay with someone always dictating what you can say or do. But I'm thankful to be clean, and I am never returning to that place."

"Well, I don't want you going back there, either," Seth said as he entered the room.

"Y'all gotta go to the grocery store, Kim. That's why I said not to get so hyped because ain't no food in this house."

I was outside sitting in my car in the parking lot of Publix at Mary Brickell Village, blasting Jay-Z's latest music while bumping my head to the beat. I was done with the whole track and on to Keyshia Cole when I noticed Keena still had not come out of the store. I called her, and she picked up the phone.

"What's taking you so long? I'm starving." I was laughing, but I was dead serious.

"Girl, I'm in line now. I'll be out in a minute."

A few minutes later, I watched as Keena walked out of the store but was suddenly stopped by two women. I didn't think anything of it until I saw her let go of the cart, and it started rolling. My antenna immediately shot up. I hopped out of my car so fast and ran toward them. By the time I got there, they were in a full-fledged fight. Keena was handling her own, but ain't no way I could sit back and let them jump my girl.

I grabbed the first girl I could get my hands on and repeatedly punched her in the face. It took her a few seconds to gather herself, but she still was no match for me. That bitch only got one damn lick in, and that was only because I looked away. I was on top of her by this time, ramming her head into the ground, and that's when she snuck in her one punch. Well, that only made her ass whooping even worse. I was mad as hell by now, and this was not even *my* fight. I felt somebody pulling me off the girl, which made me furious, and I started swinging wildly, trying to get them off me. When I realized it was Keena, I stopped.

"Come on, Kim. We should leave. You know these white people probably already called the police on us."

The way I was feeling now was fuck the police. We didn't start this shit, and I'm trying to figure out where all these fights keep coming from. We don't even know enough people here to cause problems, and this is the second damn fight Keena has had.

"What the fuck, Keena?" I said as we drove out of the parking lot. "Is there something you need to be telling me? Because why the hell are these women coming for you, or do we need to be questioning Black's ass?"

"Well, one of the girls is the girl I got in a fight with at Yardbird's. I guess she was feeling bold because she had her friend with her. That bitch better stop coming for me. I'm tired of playing with her and her fucking up my face." She was looking in the mirror the whole time she was saying this.

"Black is going to be mad as hell."

"Seth is gonna be mad too. Dang, all a bitch wanted was some home cooked food and some good dick. Is that too much to ask for?"

Keena busted out laughing. Hell, I had to laugh too because I crack my own self up at times. Even though I didn't want no nasty-ass McDonald's, I pulled up at the drive-through and ordered four Big Mac combos, then headed back to Black's house. I didn't want to cook anyway. I was trying to get Seth's ass to his house. I was *for real* in need of some dick therapy.

Black

To say I was mad when Keena and Kim walked through my door was an understatement. I'm trying to figure out who this damn girl was and why she keeps coming for Keena. At first, I thought it may have been one of my old flings who was mad because I made Keena my lady. Other than Ebony, I had not had any other girlfriends. Everybody else was just a fuck buddy. Other than a few social media pictures, nobody really knew what she looked like, and even then, I didn't announce to the world that she was my girl. Not that I was trying to keep her a secret, but with my life, I *had* to keep her a secret. I didn't want anybody coming for her. So, now, I'm starting to think there's more to it than a jealous female. I haven't given any female enough reasons even to *think* she was more than what she was.

I pulled up in my mom's driveway and saw her neighbors playing basketball outside. I threw my hand up to greet them as I got out of the car, but Quan was walking toward me before I could get into the house.

"Hey, Black, I need to talk to you about something before you leave."

I looked at him strangely because he called me Black. I know I never told that nigga my name was Black. I would have never told him that since he was my mom's neighbor, and I always kept my street life away from her and my sister.

"Why did you call me Black?"

He looked taken aback.

"Well, I know who you are and what you do, so I know that's your name."

"Nigga, you don't know nothing about me. You may have heard a few things, but you don't know nothing about me. Knowing and hearing are two different things. You only know what you heard, so for the record, my name is Peter." I walked off and left that nigga standing right there on the sidewalk. I hated bitch-ass niggas. And he's talking about what the fuck he heard. "What kind of bullshit is that?" I asked myself.

"Hey, Ma." I walked up to her and hugged her. "Where's Paulina?"

"She wants to be a cheerleader, so I signed her up for a summer camp."

"Word? Paulina wants to cheer? *That's* what's up. I'm happy to hear that. Let me know if she needs something."

"Peter, I have told you about that."

"Told me what, Ma?" Of course, I already knew what she was talking about, but I decided to play along anyway.

"Boy, you already know what I am talking about. Don't play dumb with me," she said as she popped me on my arm with the dish towel.

"No, I don't. What are you talking about?"

"I appreciate the help, but I can take care of Paulina by myself."

"I know, Ma, but I like to help you."

"I can respect that, but what were you and my neighbor talking about? I had told Seth while you were in the hospital that he had been asking about you and wanted to talk to you about something. I'm guessing Seth never talked with him."

"He told me he wanted to talk to me before I left. I didn't give him a chance to say anything else." I noticed how my mom was looking at me. "What, Ma? Why are you looking at me like that?"

"I hope you know I know when you're lying. You talked to that boy too long for you to just say you'll talk to him later, but I guess it ain't none of my business. Where's Keena?"

"She's at the house."

"Y'all staying together now?"

"No."

"Well, Keena seems to be a nice girl, and I like her, but I'm still trying to figure out what happened that night you got shot. Both of you say it was an accident, so I guess there isn't much more to say."

"Ma, for real, I still don't remember what happened that night, and it's making me mad that I can't."

"Maybe God don't want you to remember. Are you happy?"

I nodded. "I love her. In fact, I'm past loving her. I'm in love with this woman and want to marry her."

"Well, whatever happened that night, just let it go, son. I see the love you have for her all over your face."

"Oh, guess what, Ma? Seth bought Kim a brand-new Mercedes."

"He did *what? Seth?* I *know* he's for real because I can't even remember him having *one* girlfriend. I was starting to wonder about him," she said with a smirk, so I knew she was joking.

"Ma, don't play like that about Seth."

"You know I'm just messing. I love Seth like a son. Did you eat anything?"

"It doesn't matter if I did. I don't turn down food from my mom."

She walked toward the kitchen, and I was right behind her. I had already smelled the food when I walked through the door. My stomach was touching my back, I was so hungry. I didn't eat that McDonald's that the girls brought back, and I don't eat breakfast. I sat at the table as my mom put a plate of meat loaf, macaroni and cheese, greens, and mashed potatoes with gravy in front of me. I fucked that food up in less than ten minutes.

"You *were* hungry, wasn't you?"

"Yes, something like that."

"You know I can fix you another plate."

"Nah, I'm good, Ma," I said as I went to the cabinet to grab a cup to get something to drink. All I needed now was some of my mom's good ole sweet tea to finish off this meal, and I was straight.

I sat and talked to my mom for about another hour before deciding to head out. When I walked outside, I looked over at Quan. He was still playing basketball with his little brother. Even though I thought he was a bitch-ass nigga for what he said, my street intuition would not let me just get into my car. I had to find out what he wanted to talk to me about. All I knew was that he better not be on no bullshit.

"Yo, Quan. What did you have to holla at me about?"

He turned to his little brother and said something to him before he walked over toward me.

"Yo, man, I want to apologize about earlier. I had no business stepping to you like that, but anyway, that's not what I wanted to talk to you about. Do you remember when I kept saying I knew that girl you had with you?"

Now, this nigga had my ears perked up, talking about Keena.

"Yes, I remember. What's up?"

"Well, I knew that girl was not from Atlanta. I knew that I knew her."

"So, where do you know her from?" I said "her" on purpose so as not to mention her name in case he was on some bullshit. I swear this nigga was something else.

"She's from Charlotte. My girl back home was in a group home with her. I remember meeting her one time before."

"So, I'm confused about what the problem is, that she's from Charlotte."

"She told us she was from Atlanta. So, why would she lie if she doesn't have nothing to hide?"

"She said she was from Atlanta, which she may very well be. She could be from Atlanta and raised in Charlotte."

"Nah, bro, I don't think you're hearing me. That girl is something else. She's about her paper and don't care who she hurts in the process. She set niggas up along with her homegirl and robbed them blind. That's what I meant when I said she wasn't 'right.'"

When Quan said that, a lightbulb instantly went off in my head. *That* is what our argument was about that night I got shot. It was all coming back to me now. I had read a text message on her phone from some nigga named Joc. *I* was her next lick. She came to Miami to rob me. I was now furious. I'm going to murder this bitch . . . her and her friend.

"You OK, Peter?"

I had forgotten that he was still standing right here.

"Yes, I am." There was no way I could let him know that what he said fazed me at all. "Yeah, I'm good. Keena wouldn't do that to me, but I appreciate the lookout." When she popped up dead, I did not need him thinking back to this conversation, so I had to lead him to believe we were good.

"You're welcome, my nigga. You know I had to let you know the info on these hoes. These hoes ain't loyal."

"I feel you, man. Let me go. I need to get home now." I hopped into my car and sped out of my mom's driveway so fast that I left tire marks.

Joc

I was about to turn into the entrance of the Pork and Beans Projects when I spotted Lisa. Lisa is Seth's big sister. She used to be beautiful back in the day until drugs took over her world. Drugs don't discriminate. They will ruin anybody's life. Lisa looked bad as hell. I was about to hit Seth directly in his heart. Just because his sister was a junkie didn't mean he loved her even less. Lisa was his heart, and everybody knew that. At one point, most of the local dealers were scared to sell her anything out of fear of what Seth would do to them. He had made it very clear that if he caught anybody selling anything to his sister, he would kill them. Then a few dudes tested his gangster, and he made an example out of them. He killed all three of those niggas with no remorse. After that, she couldn't get any dope in Miami. She started going MIA for days because she would go to other cities in Florida to cop from. Seth got tired of hearing his nephew crying, wondering where his mom was after not hearing from her for days. Eventually, he just let it go and let niggas know it was OK and not to sell her any bad dope. Shortly after that, Seth moved his mom and nephew out of Florida. I quickly busted a U-turn in the street and rolled up on Lisa.

"What's up, Lisa?" I asked her as I rolled down my window. She put her hand over her eyes, trying to shield the sun from her face as she tried to figure out who I was.

"Do I know you?" she asked me as she bounced from foot to foot, rubbing her hands together.

"You don't remember me? We went to school together. I'm Kenneth." I told her Kenneth because she does not know me as Joc. I also had some plans for her, and I didn't want her to alert her brother. She placed her hand on her head like she was thinking about if she remembered me. I pulled some money out of my pocket and dangled it in front of her. Her eyes lit up like a Christmas tree. I knew even if she didn't remember me, that money would override it.

"Yes, I think I do remember you."

I laughed to myself. I knew she didn't remember me for real. I wasn't that popular in high school. I didn't even have the best clothes, and she was the prettiest thing walking around Booker T. Washington High School. That was the reason I started selling drugs. I got tired of my brother and me looking like bombs.

She walked over toward my car. "What do I have to do to get that money?"

She was funny as hell. I would never fuck a junkie bitch. "For starters, you can get into my car."

She opened the door and got in without any other questions.

Hours Later . . .

Lisa had just woken up after I had knocked her ass out. She looked around the room, trying to figure out where she was. She was mumbling through the tape I had over her mouth. I handed her a phone I had copped from Walmart before I snatched the tape off her mouth.

"Call your brother," I told her as I pushed the phone in her face. She looked at me all puzzled at first before she said anything.

"I don't know how to get a hold of my brother," she said as tears and snot ran down her face while she shook her head.

"Bitch, I don't care *how* you get his number. You better call your mom or something, but I'm not playing with your ass." I pulled my gun out and pushed it in her face. She grabbed the phone and started dialing a number.

"Hey, Ma." She was stuttering when she said it.

"What's wrong with you, Lisa, and how much do you need this time?"

"Ma, can I have Seth's number?"

"What do you need his number for? You didn't even ask about your son, but you want your brother's number? You don't need to be calling him asking him for nothing. He's already taking care of your son."

I could hear all this over the phone. I assumed Lisa only called her mom for money and never asked about her son. I was really starting to grow impatient now. I didn't have time for a family therapy session.

"Ma, please, not right now. Can I please just have his number?"

"Well, he is your brother, so I'm going to give it to you." After her mom recited the numbers to Seth's phone, I grabbed the phone and hung up in her ear. She was still talking, but I was not trying to hear none of that shit. Next, I dialed Seth's number and handed her the phone again. I was not surprised when he didn't answer. He's a street nigga, and she was calling from an unknown number. I texted him like I was her, telling him to call me back. A few minutes later, the phone rang.

I answered the phone and placed it to Lisa's mouth. As soon as I did that, she started screaming into the phone that I was going to kill her. I hit her in the face with my gun. "Bitch, shut the fuck up."

"Lisa! Lisa!" Seth started screaming through the phone.

"Nigga, this is *not* Lisa."

"Who the fuck is this? Nigga, you got a lot of motherfucking nerves snatching my sister. Do you know *who* you are fucking with?"

"Nigga, you have a lot of balls yapping your jaws like I don't have your sister's life in my hands."

"Nigga, you better leave my sister alone. Be a real man and come for me—not her." I let off a shot. I had to show this nigga who was running this show because he was acting like he was.

"Lisa, are you OK?"

"He shot me in my foot. Oh God, he shot me in my foot!"

"OK, man, what do you want from me?" I could hear the shakiness in his voice, like he was on the verge of tears. I knew how much that nigga loved his sister.

"Oh, now, you trying to pipe down. I don't want nothing from you. I just had to show you that you are *not* untouchable. Now, you can say goodbye to your sister. I *am* going to kill her. Before I kill her, though, I want to play a game with you. She's in an abandoned warehouse, so you do have a chance to save her. The only thing is, there are plenty of abandoned warehouses in Miami, and you only have four hours to find her. I have a bomb in this building that will go off in four hours. And even if you find her, just know I will fuck her over to the point where you won't even recognize her."

Seth got quiet. I could tell he was in panic mode. I interrupted his thoughts. "The clock has just started ticking."

Keena

I was pacing the floor when Peter walked in with a scowl on his face. I assumed he was upset about Seth's sister that neither Kim nor I even knew he had. I had just gotten off the phone with Kim, and I was listening as Seth was on the phone with an unknown person. Seth was ready to wreak havoc on the whole of Miami. I told

Kim to tell Seth we should all split up because we didn't have enough time to be riding together. He had to call in his street soldiers because the four of us would not cut it either.

"Why did you come here first instead of going out to help Seth find Lisa?"

Peter looked at me with a bewildered expression, and I knew then that the scowl he wore on his face had *nothing* to do with Lisa. I began to get a bad feeling because, obviously, that look was about me. However, whatever the look was about, Lisa's situation overrode it. He immediately dialed Seth's phone. Then he gave me some areas he wanted me to check and told me if I found her to call them and not stay near the building. He left after that.

I drove down the streets of Miami with a lot on my mind. I was worried about Seth's sister, Lisa, but the thoughts of what was on Peter's mind was bothering me. I had a feeling he was starting to remember what we had fallen out about. That had to be it because we were fine when he left the house this morning. We had not argued. I just want him to know that I do love him, and I would never hurt him.

I called Kim to see if she had heard anything about my situation, and she said that if she had, I would have already known that. After I thought about it, I knew she was right. She had just as much to lose as I did. Once Peter told Seth, he would know they were our targets.

From all the information I received from Peter, Seth had never had a girlfriend before. He said Seth had to love Kim since he just bought her that Mercedes-Benz. That would be his first heartbreak, so I know he would not hesitate to kill Kim. Kim *will* shoot something, but she is not as hard core as me. I don't give a fuck about murdering nobody, but she does.

I looked at the clock on the dashboard of Peter's car. A whole hour had already passed, which meant we only had three hours left to find his sister. I had to put my problems aside for a moment and focus on finding Lisa.

Something clicked in my head, and I realized I didn't even know what this girl looked like. So, even if I find her, how would I know it's her? So I decided to call Peter.

"What?" He picked up the phone with an attitude. I knew then that he did know. Even given the situation that was going on, Peter still would not have a nasty attitude toward me.

"I need a picture of Lisa. I don't have a clue what she looks like."

"Lisa is the least of your worries."

"Huh?" He said it so low I barely heard him, but oh, I *did* hear what he said.

"Do you have something you need to be telling me?"

"No."

"Are you sure?"

"Yes, I'm sure. Can you please just have Seth send me a picture?"

"He probably doesn't have a decent picture. Lisa has been on drugs for years." I thought that explains why we didn't know anything about her. "But I'll call Seth and have him send you a picture."

He hung up the phone without saying another word. My heart just broke into a million pieces. Peter just gave me a chance to explain myself . . . and I lied. I knew it was over for us. I picked up the phone to dial his number again, but my phone rang before I could dial it.

"Hello."

"Bitch, y'all can forget about finding Lisa. I told you I would rock your entire world and everything in it."

I was stuck on stupid. Joc was on the phone. I was in my feelings because Seth's sister might die because of something I did.

"Joc, please, tell me where she's at. I didn't even know Seth had a sister, so she's innocent. So leave her out of it. Hell, leave everybody out of it. Your beef is with me."

"No, my beef is with all of y'all. Well, Kim don't have shit to do with it either, but she's just guilty by association."

"Why would your beef be with all of us? What did they do to you? This was supposed to be a robbery, plain and simple. I fell in love with Peter and couldn't go through with it, Joc. That's all. I didn't betray you or try to keep all the money. There is no money because I couldn't go through with it. Now, tell me where Lisa is so I can save her."

"This is what you don't know, Keena. Black, or Peter as you call him, was my daddy's godson. I'm just finding all this out. I never knew who my father was, but, oh, my twin brother did."

"Your twin brother?"

"Yes, my twin brother, Turk. My brother had been talking to our dad behind my back, but he never told me. My mom never told me who my daddy was. So I grew up knowing nothing about him other than rumors I had heard."

"I'm still trying to figure out what that has to do with Peter and Seth."

"Those motherfuckers killed my brother, and then they killed my nephew a few months ago. So yes, I *am* beefing with them. You were just a pawn. I wanted to take that nigga's empire before I murked his ass."

My heart was fluttering. I had to get some information from him, but I needed to find Lisa. I would not be able to live with myself if something happened to her. I needed to call Peter, but I was afraid I wouldn't be able to get Joc back on the phone. So I pulled over on the side of the road to shoot a text message. I guess Joc must have had a change of heart because he told me that Lisa was either on the east side of Miami or the west side. That eliminated two sides, so that gave us some time. I hung up on him and immediately dialed Peter because I knew my text message was puzzling him.

"Keena, what the hell are you talking about? Who the hell is Joc?" I knew I was about to incriminate myself, but at this point, it didn't matter. I had to save that girl's life. I began to tell Peter some of the story because time was not on our side. I didn't have time to tell him everything, but he understood and agreed to talk about it later. I was not sure if he was just hurt or mad. He was obviously both because since Ebony got killed, he hadn't gotten too close to another female.

I dialed Kim's number and told her what was going on. I had to warn her because I knew Peter would tell Seth. They're best friends. I wanted her to be ready for whatever was about to come. She was upset, but she agreed with me. We couldn't let Lisa die to protect our secret. She was the innocent one in this whole situation. We knew what we were walking into if our secret got out, but she didn't.

Peter called me back after I got off the phone with Kim.

"You know I love you, right?"

"Yes, Peter. I know that you do, and I am sorry. I truly am. Please believe that I wouldn't hurt you. I gave you my virginity. That should tell you something."

"Right now, I don't know what to think, Keena. All I know right now is that my best friend, my brother, is hurting right now because he can't find his sister. I didn't call you back for that. I called you back to say go to my house and wait for me. We got this from here."

"You want me to go to your house?" I had hesitation in my voice, and he picked up on it.

"You don't have to be afraid to go there, Keena. I honestly want to do something to you, but I am willing to hear you out." He hung up the phone, and I headed to his home.

When I arrived, I didn't know if I should go into the bedroom or what. I didn't want to get too comfortable because I knew things could get ugly. I was praying on the whole ride back over here. I prayed that they found Lisa in time, but I was also praying for myself. I started to call Kim to come over to the house and wait with me, but I knew that wouldn't be a great idea. She had to face whatever wrath Seth was about to bring her way. I kind of wish I were just going through this by myself. Whatever issues Joc had with me, he was taking them out on everybody else. I know he told me something about Peter killing his brother and nephew, but I still felt responsible. If I had not let greed take over my mental thinking, none of this would even be going on right now. I looked at the time on my cell phone and noticed we only had one hour left. Quickly, I dropped down on my knees and prayed more fervently.

Chapter 31

Seth

I was hitting every abandoned warehouse I could think of until Black called and eliminated two sides of town. Beads of sweat dripped down my face, and my heart beat so loud, I could hear it pounding out of my chest. I *had* to find my sister. There was no way I could call my mom and tell her that her daughter was dead. That would kill her, and I know it would tear up my nephew. I was trying to figure out who this nigga Joc was and what beef he had with us. Black didn't tell me the whole story because time was not on our side. I had the entire hood out searching for Lisa and offered two different rewards. One was for the return of my sister, and the other one was a bounty on whoever this nigga Joc was. I knew somebody would have some information, either way.

I looked at the dashboard clock. Only twenty minutes were left, and I started to get nauseated. Time was ticking by too fast, and nobody had found her. As soon as that thought entered my mind, my phone rang. It was one of our street soldiers.

"Man, please, tell me something good." I was praying he had some good news for me.

"Well, I did find her, man, and the ambulance is on the way. It doesn't look good for her, though. She was savagely beaten. Meet us at the University of Miami Hospital."

My stomach was in knots. I didn't want to imagine what I was about to walk into. I knew I had to call my mom, but I didn't want to call her yet because I wanted to see what I was up against. I didn't want to worry her if I didn't have to. But I decided to call Kim and let her know we found Lisa and for her to meet me at the hospital. I know I had Black for support, but I needed my woman there too.

When I walked through the hospital doors, I saw doctors and nurses running around everywhere. Patients were up against the wall on gurneys. I don't know if they didn't have the space or what, but it was sad that so many people were sick or hurt. Family members were hollering and screaming because of the news they had received from the doctors.

As I hurried to the emergency room desk to get information on my sister, I heard "Code Blue, Code Blue." I never even got to speak with the lady at the desk because she threw her finger up to tell me to hold on a minute.

I glanced around the waiting room, looking for a familiar face so I could find out something. I didn't want to go off on the receptionist because I was not in a good mood. I knew I would be really ugly to her. At the same time, I felt like she was being rude to me. At first, I thought she told me to hold on because of the Code Blue thing, and I can respect that. Now, I saw that was not the case at all. This bitch was for real on a personal phone call. I walked over to the desk, snatched her cell phone right out of her hand, and threw it on the floor.

She hopped up from her chair like she was going to do something with her hands on her hips. "I *know* you didn't just break my phone." She said this while rolling her neck, and her hands were flying in the air like she wanted there to be a problem.

"Yes, the fuck I did. Now, what the fuck do you think you're going to do about it? You told me to hold on while you took a personal phone call, and my sister might be dead as we speak." She hung her head in shame. I guess she realized that she was wrong.

"I apologize, sir. You're right. I should have been more professional. I got caught up arguing with my no-good baby daddy because he won't buy our son any diapers after I had already told him I didn't have any money. I know that is *not* your problem, and again, I deeply apologize."

I reached in my pocket, pulled out a wad of money, and handed it to her. I have a soft spot for kids. The fact that she was woman enough to apologize also made me do it.

"You don't have to do that, sir. If I wasn't on my phone, it would have never got broken." I could tell she was a very humble person who was just going through an issue at the time.

"I know I don't but take it anyway. Buy you a new phone and do something nice for your son." I knew I had given almost $5,000.

"What is your sister's name, sir?"

"Lisa. Lisa Chalk." As she started typing on her computer, I turned around when I heard Kim call my name. She grabbed me and hugged me tightly.

"Sir, I'll go get the doctor for you. Wait right here until I get back."

Kim grabbed my hand and held it.

It seemed like hours passed by before the doctor came out to talk to me. But in all actuality, it had only been five minutes.

“Hello, sir,” he said as he reached his hand out to shake mine. At that moment, I knew something was not right, and my knees got weak.

“I hate to have to be the one to tell you this, but your sister didn’t make it. There was too much internal bleeding.” I don’t remember anything else that doctor said. He sounded like he was talking in a cave. I sat down because I felt weak. I didn’t want to make that phone call to my mom, but I knew I had to. I looked up when I heard Black cry out in pain. I knew he was just as hurt as I was. Lisa was all he knew. She was his big sister too, and Sarita was standing there trying to hold him up. I was wondering where Keena was because I know Kim had to have called her. She needed to be here. We were family, and I needed all the support I could get right now.

A nurse came over, showed us to a private room, and asked if I wanted to see Lisa. I looked at Kim because I needed her and Black to go in with me. I still needed to call my mom, but I was not ready yet. I was still praying this was all just a bad dream . . . a horrible nightmare. Finally, I told the nurse to give me a minute because I had to get myself together first. She understood and said she would be back shortly.

Just as we were about to go back to see my sister, Keena walked through the door. I saw Black look at her, but the look he gave her was not the same one I was used to seeing on his face when she entered a room. But now was not the time to dwell on that.

“No!” I screamed with my hands covering my mouth as I looked at my sister. They hadn’t cleaned her up yet. Blood was all in her hair and caked on the right side of her face. I was going to kill this nigga, Joc. He doesn't know *who* he's fucking with. I knew I couldn't call my mom with this news. I would have to make a trip to South Carolina to bear this news. You can't tell a mom her child is dead over the phone. I would need Black's mom to go with me. She and my mom were pretty good friends.

I saw Sarita trying to comfort Black, and I thought Keena would have been jealous, but she was not. Instead, she stood on the other side of him, trying to console him as well. That gave me a new respect for her because she knew the situation and didn't let any jealousy get in the way of it. Other females would not have cared what was going on. They would not have let no other female comfort their man.

"Keena, can you call Black's mom for me?"

"I already did. I told her to meet us at the hospital because something was going on with your sister. She should be here at any moment."

Keena

I watched everybody as they cried. My heart went out to them. I hurt for them, even though I didn't know Lisa. They said she was a drug addict, but she still didn't deserve to die like this. I felt like this was all my fault, and I knew there was no coming back from this. I didn't trip when that Sarita girl was comforting Peter. I'm cut from a different cloth than the rest of these females. I keep trying to tell people that, but nobody tries to hear me. I am not the jealous type of female. It was not the time or the place for it, anyway. I know she's been around and knew Lisa, so she had every right to be here. I admit I was a little upset about that stunt she pulled when Peter was in the hospital, but I was over it.

Peter's mom walked into the room. She hugged Peter, Seth, and even Sarita. Then she pulled back from Sarita. "Why haven't I seen you in a long time?"

"I don't have a real reason other than life."

"Did anybody call Pam?" Pam is Seth's mom.

"No. I want you to ride to South Carolina with me. I can't tell my mom this over the phone."

"I agree with you. Paulina is at cheerleading camp, so I don't have to worry about her. Pick me up from my house in about an hour. I need to freshen up and pack a bag." She left shortly after that, and we were right behind her.

When we got to the house, I asked Peter if he wanted me to ride with them. Of course, I wanted to be there for them, but I was a bit hesitant, considering everything going on. Not to mention I felt like I was partly to blame. I am not taking the entire blame for this because I think this was happening way before I even came into the picture. I just happened to be a convenient pawn.

"Go ahead and get a bag ready for us both. We'll drive one of my cars. I want to be there for my nigga, but we also have some unresolved issues. On the ride down there, we can talk, so I can decide if you're going to need a ride back . . . or not."

I looked at Peter like he was a two-headed dragon. I knew how cruel he could be, but he was never this way with me. He was always loving toward me, but this person was *not* Peter. The person standing before me was Black, and I didn't like that person. Since he wants to act like he has no sense, I think it's time he met the *real* Keena. He needed to stop trying to handle me like I was a punk or something.

"If you feel that way, I can just go back to my condo, or I could just drive my own car. There's no way in this world I will let you get me to another state and expect me to find my own way back. If I ride up there with you, then best believe, I *will* be riding back with you. You really got me fucked up, Black." I had so much attitude in my voice that he was now looking at me all sideways.

"Let's just get this over with now, and we can go our separate ways if that's what you decide is best for you. I have a lot of investments. I told you the truth about that. How I got the money to invest is a whole different story. After my father was killed, none of my family would take me in. My dad took care of his entire family, and yet, none of them would take me in. I ended up in a group home where I met Kim. Kim's mom got killed just like my dad, and we instantly clicked. I turned 18 first, and they kicked me out of the group home that same day with nothing to my name but some raggedy-ass clothes.

"The first time I robbed a nigga was not intentional. This nigga named Carlos took me in and acted like he cared about me. He told me he didn't want nothing from me; he just wanted to help me. After about two months, he started hinting that nothing in life was free, so he set me up for my first job. He sent me to a local drug dealer, then he came in and robbed him. That was a bad mistake because they ended up in a shootout and killed each other. But I walked away with everything.

"By the time Kim turned 18, I had already robbed like three niggas and had a two-bedroom apartment waiting for her when she got out of the group home. So Kim never had to be homeless. Then I put her up on game, and it was on from there.

"I met Joc through a mutual friend because I had some free dope I was trying to sell. After being around him for a while, we became friends. I admit I did have a slight crush on him, but I never took it there. He started hinting around about you, so I began to study you so I could learn your habits. You were going to be my last lick because I knew I could retire with the money I made from you. But I knew I couldn't do it once I met you and started hanging around you. I fell in love with you, and I have never been treated by any man other than my father the way you treated me. You loved me for me, and I loved you for you. When I see you, I don't see Millionaire Black. I see Ordinary Peter. I gave you my most prized possession. I gave you my virginity.

"Despite what people thought about me, I was never a whore. I don't think a virgin can be one anyway. I liked money and did not care how I got it or who got hurt in the process. My heart turned cold the day my daddy got killed, and then I met you. You made my heart warm again." I took his hand and placed it over my heart as I was saying this.

"If you want to be done with me, I understand. I know it will be hard to trust me again, so it's probably best if we go our separate ways. All I ask is one thing."

"What's that?" he asked as he cocked his head to the side, wondering what kind of favor I could possibly want from him.

"I have never seen Kim this happy. Can we just keep our problems to ourselves and let our friends be happy?"

"I can't do that."

I dropped my head when he said that. I didn't like it, but I understood. Seth was his best friend. Who was I to tell him to keep a secret like that from his best friend?

"I'll be gone by the time you get back." I turned to walk off, but he grabbed my arm. When I turned around to face him, he kissed me with so much force that my knees got weak. I grabbed the back of his head and forced my tongue down his throat. I could taste the peppermint on his tongue, which made me suck even harder. Next, I took my right hand and placed it on his dick. His dick was rock hard and standing at attention. I pulled his basketball shorts down and began to undress myself with my other hand. Then I stepped back and stared at him as I licked my lips.

His dick was simply perfect, and my pussy was soaking wet, awaiting him to penetrate me. I turned to walk off, put my finger up, and beckoned him to follow me. When I got into the room, I lay on the bed and scooted to the edge. He flipped me over and started eating me from the back. He licked me from my pussy all the way to my ass. He stuck his tongue in my ass, and I moaned loudly. This felt different, but it felt so good. I could tell he was putting his all into our lovemaking session. This was not just a fuck. I knew then that he forgave me for what I did. He bent my knees to my stomach as I enjoyed his tongue. That tongue he has should be registered because it's a deadly weapon. Of course, I didn't have anyone else to compare him to, but I knew this felt right. Then Peter flipped me on my back as he buried his head in my pussy. He was making love to me with his tongue.

Then he slowly entered me. I tensed up because he was so big. His dick was long and thick; I could see the veins popping out.

He pushed my legs back, causing me to scream because it felt so good. He was rubbing on my pussy as he pumped in and out of me. My feet were touching the headboard, and I tried to close my legs because I was starting to cramp.

"Open your legs, Keena."

"Oh, baby, I am. It feels so good." I was panting and moaning out in ecstasy. I placed my own hand down there. He was pumping so fast, that the bed board knocked against the wall, and I could feel my titties bouncing up and down. I was digging my nails all in his back. He placed his mouth on mine, and I could hear our lips smacking together. I arched my back when he flipped me over on my stomach. I was throwing my ass back to get all his dick. His balls slapped my ass, and I heard my ass clapping. I buried my face in the covers to keep from screaming.

"Don't hold back, Keena, baby; let it out."

I leaned my head back to kiss him over my shoulder, and he flipped me over and was now lying on his back, and I was riding him cowgirl style. I placed my feet flat on the bed with my hands on his knees and started bouncing on his dick. His toes began to curl as he started bucking back at me. "Fuck, Keena; damn, baby, your shit feels good." I tightened up my pussy walls, and he was about to lose his mind. He was moaning and kissing me on my ass while I continued to ride him cowgirl style backward.

"Let me know when you're about to cum, Keena. I want to see it all over my dick."

"I'm about to cum now, baby," I screamed as my legs began shaking.

"Why are you shaking?" he asked as he picked me up and placed me on the edge of the sink in the bathroom.

"This feels *so* good." Once I was on the edge of the sink, he placed my legs up there as well, so I couldn't move. He then began to pound my pussy as my head fell against the mirror. My legs *really* started to shake, and I knew I was on the verge of an orgasm. "Oh shit," I yelled as my nut began running down my leg. When he pulled his dick out, my nut was all over his dick. Finally, he helped me off the sink.

"Thank you, baby. I needed that. I do forgive you, and we *will* be all right." He leaned over to kiss me before he turned on the shower. "We need to get out of here. Seth and everyone else are waiting on us, I'm sure. We've already taken too long, but we both needed that. I haven't loved a female since Ebony, and what you were trying to do to me had my head fucked up. I loved that girl, but with you, it's different. I'm *in love* with you, and you're the one I want to spend the rest of my life with. If you have any more secrets, I suggest you tell me now. There may not be a next time. I know you think you're a gangster and all," he started laughing as he talked, "but I need you to be a woman for me. There is only room for one man in this relationship, and that's *me*. I have plenty of money so that you can cut out all that extra shit. I know you also have your own money, and you have said plenty of times how you just want me. I believe that. We'll be financially straight. I know Kim is your girl, but she can have that condominium. You're moving in here with me.

"The reason I said I cannot do that with Seth is because he already knows. He had already figured it out. He loves Kim too. She is his first real girlfriend. You know he has never really been in a relationship until now. He said no damage was done, and he doesn't blame you for his sister's death."

That made me feel better, and I began to loosen up some. "Let's go so that we can get on the road. I'm sure your mom is waiting on us." So we headed out and hopped in Peter's Range Rover Sport. I loved the color of this car because it was electric blue. Of course, it didn't help that blue was my favorite color.

"I don't know if I want you to play DJ because we got a long ride. Don't nobody want to hear all that sappy music," he said, laughing.

"I don't listen to sappy music. I like Plies and Boosie BadAzz."

"Like I said, sappy music."

"What's wrong with Plies? Plies speaks the truth."

"I ain't gonna lie. I like some of his music, but I want to hear Kodak Black," he said as he snatched the iPod out of my hand.

"Oh, hell no," I said as I snatched it back. "Don't *nobody* want to hear nothing that ugly-ass nigga got to say. It ain't but about two of his damn songs that I like." We were wrestling with the iPod as we pulled out of the driveway.

We drove up to his mom's house, and Seth was right behind us. I thought we were running late, but since we pulled up at the same time, it let me know that we were not. I saw that they had that girl Sarita with them. Now, I'm not a jealous female, but I still feel like something went on between her and Peter that they were not talking about. I'm a woman, and my woman's intuition told me something was there.

I quickly hopped out of the car because I was going to get into the backseat so Peter's mom could sit in the front. But she stopped me before I could get back inside the car. "You can stay in the front. We're going to ride with Seth." She pointed to the two of them.

She stopped and looked at me up and down before she finished talking. For the first time since being around her, I felt uncomfortable. I wonder if Peter had told her anything. All that was going through my head. I held my breath, waiting for her to finish whatever she had to say. I wished she would just say it because she was making me nervous.

"Are you pregnant? I dreamed of fish last night, and my fish dreams are *always* true."

I finally exhaled when I heard that. Her asking if I was pregnant was *not* what I wanted to hear, but it was better than her knowing I tried to rob her son. I looked around and noticed all eyes were on me, including Peter's.

"No," I said as my hand went to my stomach. Then I caught a look on Sarita's face as well. That was not an ordinary look. That was a hurt look. I made a mental note to myself to ask Peter about her on our ride to South Carolina. I was happy now that they decided to ride with Seth. His mom had me thinking, though. So much was going on that I hadn't even paid any attention to my period. But now that I think about it, I did miss my period. I didn't want to let it be known, though, because that was a private matter I should discuss with Peter first.

"You might want to get you a pregnancy test, Ms. Keena," his mom stated as she got into the car with Seth. Sarita was right behind her, looking like a lost puppy.

We pulled off, and it was quiet at first, but I could feel Peter looking at me out of the corner of his eye. Finally, I could no longer take the silence, so I broke it. "What's up, Peter?" He turned and looked at me with a smirk on his face.

"So, am I going to be a daddy?"

"Hush. I hadn't thought about my period with everything that's been going on. Now, with what your mom just said, she has me thinking. I haven't had my period. I'll get a test once we reach South Carolina. What's up with Sarita, though?"

He looked over at me as he licked his sexy-ass lips. My pussy instantly became wet, and I wanted to take him right there on the highway.

"What do you mean, what's up with her? I already told you that we grew up with her."

"No, Peter. I mean, what's *really* up? I saw her face when your mom asked me if I was pregnant. That was a look from a woman who was hurt by something. Have you ever slept with her? Of course, if you have, that was before me, but I at least think you should tell me. I don't like being made a fool of."

"Yeah."

"Yeah, what?"

"Yeah, I slept with her before. We took each other's virginity."

Now, *that* I was not expecting to hear.

"Oh," I said, holding my head down and playing with my fingernails.

"Lift your head. That was so long ago. I don't want her. Now, that is a secret that Seth doesn't even know anything about. They continued to be close, but we were not as close as before we had sex."

"I'm not worried about her. I only asked because I felt like there was more to the story. She keeps giving me these funny looks." I noticed we had gotten off the exit and no longer followed Seth. "Where are we going? Why did you get off?"

"We are going to get you a pregnancy test. There is no way I am waiting until we get to no damn South Carolina. We can catch up. I know how to get to Seth's mom's house." We pulled up to a Walgreens, and Peter hopped out of the car and told me he would be right back.

After about five minutes, he returned to the car with a bag in his hand. I assumed it was the pregnancy test. What I *didn't* understand was why he didn't just take me to the store with him so I could use the bathroom. He was so anxious to see if I was pregnant that he missed the most important part—which was me. I just looked at him as he handed me the bag.

"What are you looking at me all crazy for?"

"You left me in the car. How am I supposed to pee if you left me in the car?"

"Oh." He started laughing because he realized what he had done. "Come on and go to the bathroom."

"You *really* want me to go to the bathroom in a Walgreens to find out if I'm pregnant."

"Yes, I do."

I just laughed at him as I got out of the vehicle to enter the store.

I waited in the bathroom while watching the lines turn from one to two. I leaned against the wall trying to gather my thoughts. I was not sure what kind of a mom I would be. I didn't have a mother figure growing up. I was scared for my child because I was not even sure if I could be a great mom.

Suddenly, I was snapped out of my thoughts as I heard Peter beating on the bathroom door, asking me what was taking so long. I unlocked the door as I handed him the test. Then silently, I walked past him and headed toward the car.

We had been driving for about an hour, and neither of us spoke about the test results. I honestly didn't know how Peter felt about me being pregnant. We never discussed this because this is not anything we had thought about. Granted, we slept with each other without any protection, but we just didn't think about it. As scared as I was, abortion was not an option. I didn't believe in abortions.

"Peter, I did not mean for this to happen. But of course, I was not on any birth control because I was not sexually active. So I don't want you thinking I'm trying to trap you. I don't want to raise my baby alone, but I will if I need to." It took a few minutes for him to speak up, but he finally did.

"You already know you are not in this by yourself. I am *not* that nigga. I would never let you raise my baby by yourself. You already know who my mom is." I laughed at his statement. I did know his mom was not about to play that, this being her first grandchild.

"So, you're okay with me being pregnant?"

"Well, I have no choice in the matter, right? Even if I was not cool, the baby would be here in about seven months. The baby was not planned, but he is coming."

"He?"

"Yes, it's going to be a boy. I don't produce nothing but boys." I just shook my head at his cocky ass. "Just be sure you make an appointment when we get back. I know my mom and sister are going to be super happy." He pulled me in for an embrace as he kissed me on my lips. I looked down at my ringing phone. I should have known my happy moment would come to an end before it even got started. It was Joc's retarded ass calling my damn phone. He had a lot of nerve doing that. I looked over at Peter.

"Joc is calling my phone."

"Answer it. I want to see where this fuck nigga is at."

"What the hell do you want, Joc?"

"Is that the way you greet your friend?"

I knew then that this nigga was psycho. "Motherfucker, you are *not* my friend. I wish you would leave me alone. Something is wrong with you."

"Bitch, what the fuck ever. Where is your little boyfriend at?"

"I'm right here, motherfucker. I pray you know what you're doing. You fucked up, coming for mine."

"Nigga, both of the females you were so madly in love with came through me, including that bitch Ebony."

With the mention of Ebony's name, Peter got quiet.

"Leave Ebony's name out of your sick mouth. You don't even know her to be speaking on her."

"That's where you're wrong. I *do* know Ebony. Well, I *did* know her. How the fuck do you think she knew who the fuck *you* were?"

I looked over at Peter, and he was clenching his jaw.

"What the fuck are you talking about, nigga?"

"Oh, your precious Ebony was sent by me too. I sent her to do a job, but she fell in love with your black ass. I don't know why these women keep falling for you. I had my brother Turk kill Ebony because she wouldn't keep up her end of the bargain."

"Turk is your brother?"

"Yes, he was my twin brother at that."

"Nigga, I don't even know you, so I'm trying to figure out what you have against me."

"You killed my brother. I just told you what beef I had with you."

"Apparently, you had beef with me *before* I killed your brother."

"You killed my father too. Well, you had my father killed while he was in prison."

I thought about what he said. The only person I had killed while they were in prison was Bookie. To my understanding, Bookie didn't have any kids. If he did, he hid it well. Even though I already knew the answer, I asked him anyway just to be sure.

"Who was your father?"

"You know who the fuck my father was. Don't try to play dumb."

All I knew was that I didn't want to admit shit. He was going to have to say Bookie's name. I didn't trust this motherfucker. He could be recording our conversation for all that I knew.

"Look, Joc, or whatever the fuck your name is. I don't have time to be playing no cat-and-mouse games with you. Either you're going to tell me who the fuck your father was, or get the fuck off my girl's line."

He started laughing, thinking shit like this was funny.

"Oh, she's your girl? How the fuck can you claim her after finding out she wanted to rob you? Nigga, I cannot take you seriously. Bookie is my motherfucking daddy, nigga, but you already knew that."

"Bookie killed my daddy, nigga, so fuck him." I hung up the phone. I was done talking to him, and his world was soon to be over.

Black

I was mad as hell. I was going to murder Joc's bitch ass. I am sick of this nigga, and I'm about to end this shit before it goes any further.

"Are you okay, Peter?"

"No, I'm *not* okay. I haven't done anything to this nigga. I don't even know him, and he is coming for me." I did not say anything else for the remainder of the trip. Finally, Keena reached over and grabbed my hand as we rode in silence.

We pulled up to Ms. Pam's house. Seth's car was already there. As I walked toward the door, I could hear her hollering, letting me know they had already told her. My heart broke in two, hearing the high-pitched cries coming from her. Ms. Pam was like a second mother to me, and I knew I had to kill Joc for hurting her. Lisa was like a sister to me as well, so I was fucked up about this whole thing.

I walked right on in the door and grabbed Ms. Pam. She held on to me for dear life. I looked over at Sarita and saw how she was mean mugging Keena. I don't know what that was about, but I planned to check her on that shit. Keena has not shown her ass, and I was happy about that.

Now was *not* the time for Sarita to be acting like this. She knows we will never be again. I will never forgive her for killing my baby. I left that part out when I told Keena about Sarita on purpose. I have never told anybody that, not even my mom. I didn't want Keena to feel uncomfortable.

Seth made his mom pack a bag for her and his nephew. He wanted her to come with us back to Miami. The funeral was going to be there anyway because that's where we're from. I let Seth drive my Range Rover back because it had more room. I did not want Sarita riding with us because she was on one. So that was another reason I let him take my truck. I knew Keena wouldn't be able to keep her cool but for so long. Sarita was not a fighter, so I don't understand why she kept testing Keena. I don't know if she thought I would not let Keena fight her or what. I mean, real talk, I don't want the drama, but if she kept it up, I knew it could get ugly. Keena is pregnant, so ain't no way I would let her fight, but Kim would for sure back her up. Little did Sarita know these girls were about that life. Sarita was sheltered. She never had a hard life. All Keena and Kim knew was how to survive.

I thought back to the last two fights Keena had been in. I knew Joc sent that girl to fight her. The second time it was probably the girl on her own trying to get her face back since Keena had whipped her ass. Hearing that Ebony was trying to set me up was still weighing heavy on my mind. I was fucked up about what Joc said. Not Ebony . . . Man, this could not be real. I wanted to drive to Georgia, dig her ass up, and ask her why. I never saw that in Ebony. That girl loved my dirty drawers. I thought back to the day I met her.

I was a frequent visitor of Fam U. I wasn't rocking with Sarita like that, but I would check on her occasionally to make sure she was doing okay. She didn't know I was checking on her, though. I was checking out all the females, just let me be honest. They had some of the baddest females right there on campus. They had beauty *and* brains. That was the best of both worlds if you ask me.

I had bumped into Ebony because I was not paying attention to what I was doing and knocked her stuff out of her hand.

"Damn, baby girl," I said as I reached over to help her get her things off the ground.

"You may need to watch where you're going." For the first time, I looked at her face; this girl was beautiful. She had that natural beauty too. She didn't have on any makeup or anything.

"Has anybody ever told you how beautiful you are?"

"You are so lame," she said as she started laughing. "Is that the best *pickup line you have?"*

"Honestly, it was not a pickup line. You are beautiful." She started blushing. I walked away from her and went on about my day. The next day, I saw her again, and I just knew it had to be fate. This was a big campus, and

this was the first time I had ever seen the same girl twice. She was standing outside the bookstore venting to her friend about how she didn't have enough money on her book voucher to cover her books. I walked up to her and told her to follow me. She looked up at me.

"Oh, it's you again." She had a big-ass smile on her face. I grabbed her hand and pulled her along with me. "Why are you taking me into this bookstore? Do you want a T-shirt or something because we don't get a student discount? I don't think you need a discount anyway," she said as she looked me up and down. I was decked out in my polo, even down to my shoes. A big-faced Rolex sat on my wrist, and my pinky ring was blinged out.

"Girl, quit talking so much and come on." When we finally entered the store, I told her to get the rest of her books.

"Are you serious? You don't have to do that. You don't even know me."

"I know I don't know you, but I'm trying to get to know you. If I can drop bands on top of bands on strippers, I know I can buy you some books. You're in school trying to do something with your life. What kind of nigga would I be knowing I could have helped you?" We were inseparable after that.

A thought suddenly crossed my mind. Ebony had a diary that I kept over the years. I never read it because I didn't want to violate her privacy like that. But fuck that shit now. I was reading it when I got home. I needed some closure.

"You mighty quiet over there. Are you all right?"

I looked over at Keena as I slowly shook my head. "I'm still thinking about what that nigga Joc said about Ebony. I'm sorry, Keena, but I'm fucked up about this. I cannot just pick up the phone and call Ebony to get her side of the story. She's dead, Keena. That motherfucker had her killed. Didn't you hear him?" I hit the steering wheel with my fist. I was fucked up badly. "I'm going to kill him for real."

The Funeral

I was sitting around Seth's living room, looking at everybody as we were awaiting the limos to take us to the church. The funeral was being held at Mount Zion Baptist Church. I didn't realize Lisa had this much love from the city. She was a sweet person.

Lisa was very giving and would give you the shirt off her back. But unfortunately, drugs took over her life, and we all know drugs don't discriminate. Drugs will make you flip on your own kids. I noticed a change in Lisa before Seth did. He was not trying to hear it. Not his sister that he grew up with. He felt that there was no way she was snorting powder. But he finally had to face reality. It was all over the hood how pretty-ass Lisa was now getting high. Seth would not let anybody sell shit to her, but after a while, that got old too. I was snapped out of my thoughts when Seth walked over to me.

"The cars are here. Let's get ready to roll to the church."

I pulled my Gucci shades on my face and stood to my feet to walk out that door. I looked at the cars as I was about to approach them. We had five stretch Hummer limos for the family. We didn't spare any expenses when it came to this funeral. We even had a horse and carriage to take Lisa's body from the church to the graveyard.

Somehow, I started to get a funny feeling the closer we got to the church. Something just didn't feel right. I checked my sock and side to ensure both my guns were intact. I looked over at Seth. I didn't want to upset him even more than he was, but I had to ask him. This funny feeling just would not go away. "Are you strapped?"

"I stay strapped, but what's up? Why did you ask me that?"

"Something just don't feel right." I looked over at Keena. We still hadn't told anybody that she was pregnant. She hadn't even told Kim. We were waiting until the right time. She had gone to the doctor, and he confirmed that she was indeed pregnant. She was eight weeks along. I was still in shock, but I couldn't wait to be a daddy. I knew I had to take care of this Joc situation first, though. I didn't want anybody else to get hurt.

We formed a double line outside the church. Seth and his mom, along with his nephew, were first. His nephew was not taking it too well. He had been crying nonstop at the thought of not seeing his mom again. I grabbed Keena's hand, and we walked into the church. I walked by Lisa's casket. She looked so peaceful in the all-white casket with white doves engraved on the side. I reached out to touch her face. For some reason, I was expecting her to be cold, but she was not. Then I walked to my seat.

I was sitting on the pew with my head down as the tears rolled down my face. Suddenly, I looked up because I heard Pam hollering and screaming. She had walked back up to the casket.

"Not my baby. Lord, please, tell me this is a dream. This cannot be my baby lying in this casket. I am *not* supposed to bury my child. Lord, please." Watching her break down was sad. Seth walked up to her and hugged her. He was breaking down too. Keena was rubbing my back as I just sat there in a daze.

Suddenly, I heard the doors open in the back of the church. Before I could even turn around, I heard a loud sound. *Boom! Boom! Boom!* It sounded like an AK-47. I immediately grabbed Keena to cover her as I reached for my Glock 27 from my ankle. I knew this day would not go as smoothly as it should have. I started firing. There were too many niggas, and this gun only had nine rounds. My 9-mm pistol that was on my hip held nineteen rounds.

"Don't move. Stay right here," I told Keena as I looked around for my mom and little sister. So much chaos was happening, and people ran around trying to get out of the church. I heard one of the older ladies in the church ask who would do such a thing in a place of worship. I agreed with her, but I knew street niggas didn't have a heart. They would kill their own mom if she crossed them.

I was too busy crawling around on the floor, trying to make sure everybody was good that I didn't even see that nigga creep up on me. I heard the gun as he cocked it back, and I knew there was nothing I could do about it. Damn, I didn't want to die like this. I thought about my unborn child, whom I would never get to meet. I also thought about how I would be leaving Keena out here to raise our child alone. I had just promised her that she was not in this by herself. What was my mom going to do? She would go crazy without me. I waited . . . and waited for the bullet to pierce my body, but it never came.

Finally, I opened my eyes and saw this big-ass nigga standing over me fall to the ground. Keena was directly behind him. She had just put a bullet in the back of his head. I knew she was about that life, but she just proved to a nigga that she had my back. That right there was some real gangsta shit. She's pregnant, and I didn't want her busting no guns, but we were outnumbered. I looked toward the front of the church, still looking for Seth, but he was nowhere in sight. Then I saw Kim with a gun in her hand. She was shooting like a damn pro. I underestimated these girls. They were real out here.

"Pop! Pop!" That was the sound coming from Kim's gun as she shot this nigga named Dino that I knew from the hood. All I was trying to figure out was what he had against us. As far as I knew, we were cool. Next, I saw an unfamiliar nigga approach, and I heard Keena's gun again, only this time, she took off behind this nigga, and I was right behind her. There was no way in the hell I would let her do a foot chase with this nigga.

As I hopped up, pain shot through my leg. I looked down and saw red running down into my shoes. I knew I had been hit, but that would not stop me from running behind Keena.

By the time I got outside the church doors, I had heard sirens in the distance. "Keena!" She didn't stop at first. She acted as if she didn't hear me. "Keena! Don't make me call your damn name anymore." Finally, she stopped dead in her tracks. I had base in my voice, and she knew I was not playing with her.

"Peter, that's Joc. We need to get him; we just have to," she said with tears in her eyes. "Too many people have already gotten hurt."

"I'm going to get him, I promise. But we should get rid of these. I know you hear the sirens. There's no need to run because this is Lisa's funeral, so we cannot lie and say we were not here." I knew Seth would handle things on his side, so I was not even worried about him.

When we walked back around to the church after hiding the guns, the police arrived. They had the church taped up, and ambulances and fire trucks were also there. I still didn't see Seth, so I ran up to Kim. My mom, sister, Sarita, and Ms. Pam stood to my left.

"Where's Seth?" I asked Kim as I reached her.

"I don't know. I was praying he was with you. When the shooting started, he dived on top of me, and that's the last time I saw him. I pulled out my gun because I knew y'all was outnumbered, and there was no way I could just sit back and watch that."

I overheard the police say there were two fatalities, one female and one male, so my ears perked up. Another bad feeling washed over me. I ran up to the police line, trying to bust through but was stopped by the cops.

"Sir, you cannot go in there." I was still trying to get through. "Sir, do you realize you're bleeding?" I had totally forgotten about my leg.

"I don't need no motherfucking help. I need to get in that church." I could hear Keena hollering for me to calm down before they shot me. I grabbed my cell phone and dialed Seth's number. He didn't pick up, so I immediately dialed it again. I then started sending text messages. By this time, everyone had walked over toward me.

"Peter, where's my son?" I could hear the pain in her voice. I was at a loss for words. I tried to talk, but the words just wouldn't come out.

"I don't know, Ms. Pam. I just don't know." My voice was cracking as I was speaking. Suddenly, I heard Kim holler as she ran toward a gurney. All I saw was an arm hanging out because the rest of the body was covered up. I couldn't understand what she was running over there for . . . until I noticed the watch. Then I knew it was Seth. We had matching watches. So, I knew without a shadow of a doubt that was my nigga. My knees got weak, but I didn't let that stop me from running over to that gurney behind Kim. I wasted no time pulling that sheet back and saw a bullet hole in the middle of my nigga's forehead. I silently made a vow to kill every fucking body that was involved in this shit.

"No! No!" Ms. Pam's hand covered her mouth as she ran over to join me with everybody in tow.

This motherfucker better be ready to go to war with me. I planned to go to Pork and Beans and shoot up everything. I looked around for my car, then realized I didn't drive, so I ran to one of the limos.

"Get the fuck out of the car."

"Sir, I can't do that."

This motherfucker must think I'm playing with his ass. My best friend was gone, man. He's never coming back. I reached behind my back and pulled out my gun that I even forgot I had. I thought I only had two with me today, but I had three. I placed the gun in his face.

"What can't you do?" I asked him through clenched teeth.

He threw his hands up in surrender. "Sir, I know you see all those police officers over there. You will never get away with this."

"Do I look like I give two fucks about the police? My best friend was murdered in that church."

He nodded his head and walked off. I drove straight to one of our trap houses. I had a whole gun store over there. I was on a suicide mission and didn't care anything about it. I was a one-man army. As I was driving, my phone rang back-to-back. I knew it was either my mom or Keena. But right now, I didn't want to talk to either of them.

I pulled up at the trap house on two wheels. My crew ran out with guns drawn because they thought it was a robbery. I jumped out to let them know it was me. I knew they were trained to go and would not hesitate to shoot up this car. I looked over at this little nigga named Juice, who had the most heart out of the whole crew.

"Help me put these guns in the car."

He hesitated at first, but then he started walking. He looked me in the face. I'm sure he saw the tears staining my face, but at this point, I didn't care. My nigga was gone, and that was the only nigga that mattered what he thought about me.

"You all right, Black?"

"No, I am not all right. Can you just help me?"

"You know I got you. Where's Seth?"

When he asked me about Seth, I broke down. I didn't want these niggas to see me have a weak moment, but at this point, I didn't care.

"Dead."

He looked at me. I guess he wanted to see if I was serious.

"What do you mean he's dead? I thought y'all was at his sister's funeral."

"Those niggas from Pork and Beans came and shot up the funeral. Now, I'm headed over there to tear that motherfucker apart. I don't give a damn who gets hit. They didn't have no fucking respect. They disrespected Lisa's funeral like she wasn't shit, and my nigga got killed in the crossfire."

"You know we can't let you ride by yourself. We're family, and we're in this together. I also need you to produce a plan because the way you're thinking now is reckless. You definitely can't drive that big-ass car over there, drawing attention to yourself." He chuckled as he pointed at the stretch Hummer. "I'm going to send one of these peewees to drop it off where it came from before the police be looking for it. You know those crackers are going to want their shit back."

I sat down and got myself together. My phone was still ringing, and I had yet to look at it. I knew who it was, and I didn't need anybody trying to talk me out of what I knew I needed to do. I had to kill those niggas so Seth could rest in peace. If I were lying on that cold slab, I knew my nigga would do the same for me. I looked at the numerous text messages that Keena sent and finally decided to respond to let her know I was okay.

Peter: No, I am not all right. My best friend is dead, but I'm safe.

Wifey: Bae, I know you're hurt right now, and thank you for responding to me. You know I'm in the street too, so just come back home safe to me.

Peter: I will, bae. Kiss Ms. Pam for me. Keep everybody around you and Kim. I already know y'all two can handle y'all own.

Wifey: Sarita too?

I laughed at that text message because I knew Sarita had been fucking with Keena lately, and Keena was not feeling that. I knew I had to keep her safe, though. I was praying she had some get right . . . or Keena and Kim were going to kill her.

Peter: Yes, bae. Please, do that for me.

Wifey: If she starts popping off, that's her ass, and you got some making up to do.

Peter: lol. You know I got you. I love you.

Keena: I love you too.

I knew I had me a rider with Keena. I was skeptical at first because of what had happened between us. I forgive her, though, because she didn't go through with it, and she told me the truth about it. But I was worried about Ms. Pam and Kim. I knew Kim loved my friend, and now Ms. Pam has lost both of her kids. What Keena said was heavy on my mind. She said to come back home safe to her. I told her I would, and that's a promise I planned to keep.

Chapter 32

Joc

I felt triumphant after shooting up Lisa's funeral. Black thought he was sitting on top of the world, so I had to bring him down a few notches. He thought it was cool to talk all that shit on the phone. Nigga talking about getting off his girl's line. I cannot take that nigga serious. How the fuck does he think it's cool when that bitch wanted to rob him? I could only shake my head at that motherfucker.

I knew Seth was dead, and I didn't feel any remorse at all for the nigga. I already knew Black was coming for me, and he knew what I looked like. But I was ready for his ass. I lost a few good niggas too, but I ain't hurt by their deaths. They didn't mean shit to me. I honestly didn't care about nobody but myself. Everybody that meant something to me is now six feet under, and Keena might as well be dead too. I couldn't wait to kill that bitch real slow. I would make her suffer for trying to play me. I saw the way she was busting her gun, though. I underestimated her. She said she was about that life, so I guess she was right. I saw how she handled ole girl at the restaurant. That shit was gangsta as hell when she whipped out her gun and pistol-whipped her.

I thought back to the day I met Keena. She stepped out of her car in her six-inch Red Bottoms and some skinny jeans. She had on a polo tank top. Her hair was flowing down her back, and it was bone straight. What really got me was it was all her hair. I looked for the tracks but never saw any. Her lips were popping with a real light pink lip gloss. She was the prettiest girl I had seen since Ebony. My dick got hard at the sight of her, and I knew she had to be mine. I was already staking my claim on her.

I knew Keena was different, and she was feeling me too. Well, she was until Black's punk ass came into the picture. I just don't know what she sees in him that she doesn't see in me. Of course, I had money too, even though I didn't have as much as that nigga, but she wouldn't have had to worry about anything. I would have taken care of her.

I laughed as I tried to imagine the look on Black's face when he found out Ebony was not as sweet as he thought she was. I knew I crushed that nigga's heart. I hope he doesn't think running into Ebony two days in a row was a mere coincidence. I set that shit up and was closer to getting him. Ebony had the code to his safe, where he kept all his personal items like his account numbers. All I needed was his account numbers, and I would have all his money wired out of his account and into mine. Yes, I know y'all thought I was going to rob him of some in-person cash, but no, it was nothing like that. This nigga is smart. He invested his money and kept it in the bank. The day Ebony told me she was in love with him and couldn't do it was the day she signed her own death certificate. I could no longer let her breathe. Even with a gun to her head, that bitch would not flip on Black. She was loyal to that nigga.

I looked over at my cell phone because it had just alerted me that I had a text message. I was not surprised when I saw it was from Keena. I laughed at the message. This bitch thinks she's a nigga.

Keena: You know you have fucked up, don't you?

Joc: Bitch, fuck you. Don't get too comfortable because I'm going to kill you too.

Keena: Nigga, fuck you too. You're a sick bastard, and I hate the day I ever met your bitch ass.

I threw my phone back on the bed. I didn't have shit else to say to that stupid bitch. My phone went off again, only this time it rang. It was from one of my corner boys.

"Yo, what's up?" I said as I answered the phone.

"Joc, what the fuck is going on?"

My ears perked up because I didn't have a clue about what he was saying.

"Black and his niggas are over here wrecking shop. They're killing everybody they see, and they're looking for you."

"He can't be looking too hard because I ain't hiding."

"Man, you need to get over here. They're blowing up shit and everything."

"I ain't coming over nowhere. Man, fuck that nigga." I meant what I said. Fuck that nigga. I don't care anything about those niggas over in Pork and Beans. That wasn't affecting me. I hope that nigga didn't think he was hurting me by killing them because he wasn't.

"You mean to tell me you ain't coming over here? This shit right here is your business. You got this shit started, and now you're hiding."

"Nigga, I am *not* hiding. I just don't give a fuck about what he's doing. This shit doesn't concern me. All y'all motherfuckers got me fucked up. If he wants me so bad, he needs to come to *my* house and get me." I hung up the phone on that nigga. If he's going to mess around, I'm going to kill his ass for coming at me like that.

Kim

I was all cried out at this point and didn't think I had anything left. I was crying so hard I was hyperventilating and throwing up everywhere. I haven't felt this way since my mother got killed. I feel so lost without Seth. Life is just not fair. I feel like I was cheated. Just when I found a reason to live again, happiness was snatched away from me.

I looked over at Ms. Pam, and she was a zombie. I had just met her, but my heart also went out to her. At this point, I wanted to find Joc and take his ass up out of here.

"Here, drink this."

I looked up at Keena as she handed me a Coke and some crackers to settle my stomach. I didn't even think I could keep that down, so I declined it.

"I'm not going to be able to keep that down. Keena, but thank you."

"You have to eat something, Kim, or you'll be sick."

"I can't eat nothing, Keena. I feel like my heart has been ripped out of my chest. I'm hurting so bad, and it's just not fair. I can't even explain this feeling, but I don't wish this feeling on my worst enemy."

"You just met Seth, so I don't know why you're acting like you are so damn hurt. I been knowing him all my life, and not one time has *anybody* asked me how *I* feel."

That was Sarita talking, and if this bitch knew what was good for her, she would go sit the fuck down somewhere. I don't even know why this bitch is here, but she's got me fucked up. I gave her a murderous stare before I said anything.

"Bitch, why are you even here?" I made hand gestures toward the house. "How the fuck is you going to tell me how *I* feel? You don't even know me. I am not trying to tell you how to feel. I didn't know there was a damn time limit on feelings. Seth showed me what real love is supposed to feel like, and since he was 26 years old, and I'm his first girlfriend, that says a lot about how he felt about me—not that I need to explain anything to you, bitch."

I looked over at Peter's and Seth's moms and saw the look of disgust on their faces. I didn't mean to disrespect them, but I didn't give a damn at this point. I was so over this whole scene. If Keena wanted to sit and continue to babysit this disrespectful bitch, then she could. I was about to be out of this house. As I was getting my stuff together to leave, Ms. Pam stopped me.

"Kim, wait a minute. Sarita, you were way out of line for talking to Kim like that. If Seth were here, you wouldn't have said none of that. Now, I don't know where all of this is coming from, but I do know that my son loved himself some Kim. She is right when she said that he made her his girlfriend, which says a lot. Considering everything going on, Keena and Peter were nice enough to invite you to their home so you could be safe. If you want to stay here, I suggest you act like you have some sense."

To say I was shocked was an understatement. I just knew that look of disgust was for me. I guess I thought wrong. But I was done with the conversation, and I was still leaving. I didn't need any damn protection. I could protect myself.

"Thank you, Ms. Pam, for taking up for me. But I'm still going to excuse myself because I need some time alone. This is just too much for me to process."

***

It was after midnight as I made my way through the parking lot of Joc's condo. I know that nigga thought he was untouchable, thinking nobody knew where he stayed, but I spotted him at a light a few days ago and followed him here. I'm glad that I did because I was about to kill his ass by myself. I didn't need any help. The love I have for Seth was enough to push me over the edge, knowing I would never see or hear him again.

I knew breaking into Joc's condo would not be easy because of all the high-tech security surrounding the building, but I was determined. This needed to be done tonight. I had already blacked out the cameras in the parking garage and the outside ones. So all I had left to do was gain access to the building.

I waited in my car for a good forty minutes looking for someone to go into the building so I could get in too. A young white girl, probably around 18 or 19, finally pulled up with her boyfriend. I knew it was her boyfriend because I overheard her say he could spend the night because her parents were out of town. I laughed, wondering what type of teenager I would have been if my mom had lived to see it.

I slid into the elevator just as it was closing and watched the white girl as she punched in a code to get to her condo. Each condo had a name beside it, so I looked for Joc's.

"Can I press a floor for you?" she asked politely.

I shook my head no because I didn't need any witness remembering that she had pushed a button for somebody once his body was found. While she was so engrossed with her boyfriend, I hit the button for Joc's floor. The loving couple got off before I did and hadn't paid further attention to me.

I pulled my hoodie over my head as I stepped off the elevator and headed toward the camera. I blacked out the camera that was in the hallway, pointing at his door. I had to pick his locks and didn't want to be on camera.

I was grateful it was dark as hell once I was inside. I knew Joc was in there because I could hear him snoring in the back of the crib. I checked my gun and ensured I had my silencer on, but I was unexpectedly stopped dead in my tracks. Somebody else was in his place because I heard something coming from the kitchen. I knew it wasn't Joc because he snored like a grizzly bear. I knelt beside the couch when I saw a dark figure run across. I pointed my gun at the figure . . . until I saw an infrared dot pointed toward my forehead.

"Bitch, I advise you to put your gun down now."

I was frozen because this was supposed to be an easy kill. I was supposed to be in and out. I should have known this nigga was not here by himself. I put my hands in the air while my gun was still hanging on my finger. I didn't want it to fall to the floor for fear of it going off or Joc hearing it hit the floor. I had a better chance with one nigga versus two.

"Wait a minute—Kim?"

I looked up once the unknown person said my name and realized it was Peter. He lowered his gun, and I slowly got up.

"What are you doing here?" he asked me in a whisper. It was a dumb question to me. He should know I'm there for the same reason he's here—to kill Joc's punk ass. There is no way that nigga would continue to breathe after today because the other piece of my heart was gone.

Peter let out a light chuckle. "I should have known better. You *really* about that life. Well, let's do this together." I turned around too quickly and knocked the glass table over, causing it to crash to the floor. The noise was so loud it woke Joc. It didn't matter, though, because we were going to light up his ass. He just didn't know it yet.

"Who's here?" He entered the living room, rubbing his right eye with one hand and his gun in the other.

"It's the Grim Reaper, motherfucker," Peter said as he shot the gun out of his hand. I was impressed at how good of a shot he was. Joc looked shocked to see us standing in the middle of his living room like we owned the shit and paid bills here.

"What the fuck do y'all want? Get the fuck out of my house before I kill both of you." This time, it was *my* turn to laugh. It was not a funny laugh but a laugh of death because I was tired of him thinking somebody was playing with his ass.

"You're talking a lot of shit for someone about to die," I told him through clenched teeth.

"Bitch, you have some motherfucking nerve acting like you cared about that nigga."

I was through going back and forth with him. If Peter wanted to continue this charade, then that was on him. But I didn't want just to kill him, though. That was too easy. I wanted to make him suffer. I shot him in both kneecaps and watched as he fell to the ground. Peter didn't do anything to try to stop me. He just watched me work. I walked toward Joc, still aiming my gun as I kicked his gun away from him. Right after that, I shot his hands at close range as I leaned toward him so he could hear me very clearly.

"I don't know why you came for Seth, but you fucked up. I will make you suffer for every tear I have cried since Seth took his last breath." I looked down at his dick. He wore a pair of silk boxers. I pulled out the scalpel that I had taken from the hospital. I saw how big Joc's eyes got once he realized what I held in my hand.

"Oh, cat got your tongue now?"

I heard Peter say how I was really a gangsta bitch. Then he said, "Kim, you are crazy," as he watched in sheer amazement. But he hadn't seen anything yet.

I grabbed Joc's dick and sliced it off quickly, and he screamed out like a li'l bitch along with Peter.

"What the hell are *you* screaming for?" I asked Peter as I turned to look at him, confused.

"I know that shit got to hurt, girl. I hollered at the damn thought of it all."

"My *dick?* Bitch, are you *crazy?*" Joc uttered with such venom and pain.

"Oh, so you still want to talk shit and call me all out my name. To answer your question, yes, I *am* crazy. I lost all my sense earlier today." Then I grabbed his bloody, cut-off dick and forced it in his mouth. "Eat your bitch ass," I said as I stood up and shot that nigga between his eyes.

"Come on, Peter, let's get out of here."

Peter didn't say anything as he followed me out the door.

"That was some gangster shit, Kim," Peter said as we got on the elevator. "I didn't know you had all that in you, but thank you."

"You don't have to thank me; Seth is the other half of me."

"The cleanup crew will be here before you can even make it back to my house, so you don't have to worry about what happened. No body, no crime." We got off the elevator and went our separate ways.

Chapter 33

Keena

It was after two in the morning, and I couldn't get Kim or Peter on the phone. I was pacing back and forth downstairs with my phone clenched in my hand. I was worried sick and wondered where the hell Kim had run off to. I knew what Peter was up to, but I didn't have a clue about what Kim had going on. This was not like her not answering her phone when something happened. She knows that I'll worry about her.

I ran over to Peter as the door swung open, threw my arms around him, and started raining kisses all over his face. "I don't know where Kim is, and I'm worried about her. Sarita said something smart at the mouth, and Kim just up and left, talking about she needed some space."

"Kim is okay. She should be right behind me."

I already knew what was up when he said that—no other words needed to be spoken. I knew what it was when he said Kim was okay. I knew they had taken care of Joc.

The following day, I woke up to the smell of a home cooked breakfast. I walked into the kitchen, and everyone was there, including Peter. The smell of the bacon suddenly nauseated me, and I raced to the downstairs bathroom.

"I don't care what that girl says. I *know* she's pregnant, and y'all need to get her tested," I heard Peter's mom say as I ran out of the kitchen.

"She *is* pregnant, Ma. We had a test done. We were going to tell you, but so much stuff kept happening. There was just never a right time."

"You mean to tell me I'm going to be a grandma? Oh, I'm *so* excited. Pam, I am going to be a grandma."

"Congratulations," I heard her say with a hint of sadness.

"Oh, Pam, I am *so* sorry. Here I am all excited, and you just buried one child and are about to bury another one."

"It's okay. I *am* excited for you. This is your first grandbaby."

"Oh no, this is *not* her first grandbaby." That was Sarita talking.

I was now making my way back toward the kitchen because I was curious about how this was not her first grandbaby. Paulina didn't have any kids, and she was the only sibling I knew Peter had. When I walked into the room, it was suddenly as if an elephant was there. Everybody got quiet, and all eyes were on me. I cut my eyes over at Peter, who couldn't even look at me. That alone let me know that I was about to hear some shit that I didn't want to hear.

With my hands on my hips, I looked at Peter first. "What is she talking about? I am so sick of this bitch I don't know what in the world to do. She pops up out of the blue and has been coming for me ever since."

"Tell her what I am talking about, Peter." Sarita had so much bass in her voice and a smirk on her face that I wanted to smack right off. Instead, I stood there bouncing from foot to foot, awaiting my answer.

"What is she talking about?" I repeated it this time with more attitude because I was two seconds from kicking this bitch's ass by now. I couldn't even be happy about my damn pregnancy because of this hating-ass bitch. I looked over at Kim, and I knew my best friend. I didn't even have to do anything because she was ready to get her.

I guess Peter took too long to answer the question because Sarita blurted it out. "Tell her how I was pregnant with your child." Now, Peter finally found his voice.

"Sarita, I honestly don't know what your issue is. Keena is right. You have been in your feelings since I was in the hospital. Yes, we have known each other for a long time, but let's not get it twisted. We haven't been close in a long time. You always stayed in contact with Seth. I should have gotten you straight the first time you came for Keena because *nobody* will disrespect my woman. I told Keena to be cordial toward you because a lot was going on.

"Real talk, Sarita, you are *not* ready for Keena. You are not about that life; trust me when I tell you, she is the female version of me. Without saying anything else, you already know what I mean when I say that." He then turned and looked at me. "I should have told you the whole truth about what happened between Sarita and me. Yes, she was pregnant with my child, but she chose to abort my child." After saying that, he bent over and kissed my stomach.

"It doesn't matter what went on in either of our pasts. You have shown me that you are there for me. Regardless of our rocky start, I love you. I know we haven't been together that long, but I do know that I want to spend the rest of my life with you. Time can't measure our love. You are about to have my baby, and I thank you for that."

I was in tears by this time, but they were happy tears. I was praying he was going to ask me what I was thinking he was going to ask.

"I don't have a ring yet because this was so unplanned, but will you marry me?" I had my hand over my mouth as I vigorously nodded my head, trying to say yes, but nothing would come out.

Kim walked over to me and hugged me. I saw Sarita gather her things together before leaving, but Peter stopped her.

"Sarita, I know how close you were to Seth. I wouldn't dare stop you from coming to the funeral. Once the funeral is over, though, I would prefer that you stay away from me. Yes, you were pregnant by me first, but it is irrelevant since there is no baby."

"Did you know I haven't been with another man since you? I waited on you to forgive me so we could finally be a couple. Now, you parade this bitch in my face like I ain't shit."

"Sarita, that's what *you* chose to do—" but before Peter could finish talking, I slapped the taste out of that bitch's mouth. She is light-skinned, so her face immediately turned red. Her lip began to swell and bleed as she held her mouth. Peter grabbed my arm to calm me down. His touch alone gave me a sense of calmness.

"Bitch, get the fuck out of my house," I told her as I pointed at the door. "You are *never* welcomed in this house again," I said as I pushed her in the back toward the door.

"That bitch got some issues," Kim said while shaking her head.

I started laughing because I knew she was quoting Plies's song. Kim could be really retarded sometimes, but that is my bestie, and I *needed* that laugh.

Black

I was still trying to process these last seventy-two hours because shit was real. I don't know why Sarita waited years to release her skeletons, but I had no respect for that. I still can't believe my best friend, my brother from another mother, was gone. I didn't know how I would go on with the rest of my life without my right-hand man. We were supposed to raise our kids together. We talked about retiring and going on fishing trips. This was not supposed to be how my nigga left this world.

I only had peace because I knew the nigga that killed him was no longer breathing. I didn't realize how gangster Keena and Kim were until all this stuff started happening. I hate this for Kim because she was in love with my nigga. I would always make sure she was straight, though, so she didn't have to worry about anything. I plan to make sure she gets to stay in his house. Ms. Pam is not like that, though, so she would be straight.

Asking Keena to marry me even surprised me. I knew it was the right thing to do because she has been here for me through it all. I can't wait to be a father. Right now, I'm riding shotgun with Keena and Kim, heading to the funeral home. Ms. Pam asked us if we minded handling the funeral arrangements because she didn't have the strength to do it again, especially this soon. We ended up having a private graveside service for Lisa yesterday since her funeral was shot up.

I wanted to do a private graveside service for Seth, but I knew all the homies wanted to show their respect. Since the "problem" was taken care of, I doubted we would have any further difficulties.

After being at the funeral home for what seemed like hours, we finally settled on a casket and a date for the funeral. I was dressing my nigga in all-white Versace. His coffin was all white and trimmed in gold. I was sending him away just like I knew if he stepped out, that's how he would look. I wanted him to have on some of his jewelry.

I had Keena send our pictures from my phone to Walgreens so they could be printed. I was having a whole book made for his obituary. I got pictures from childhood until he took his last breath. This was my nigga, so money didn't matter.

The Burial

I looked up at the sky as I stepped out of the limo. The sun was beaming down on my face. I was looking for a sign or something just to let me know everything was going to be all right. Keena placed her hand on the small of my back for comfort. Little did she know I needed that to get past this final step of Seth's funeral. I was not ready to say goodbye. I knew this was the finale. There was no coming back from this, and it was a hard pill for me to swallow. The funeral home workers were already getting the casket out of the hearse, so I walked toward the burial plot.

I looked around at the many faces as the preacher said, "ashes to ashes, dust to dust." Seth brought out the whole city for his funeral. It warmed my heart to know that they had so much love for him.

Chapter 34

Kim

I stood at the burial plot watching them lower Seth's body into the ground. I wanted to jump into that hole with him because I felt I had nothing else left to live for. The other half of my heart was being buried right along with him. Killing Joc didn't make me feel any better because at the end of the day . . . Seth was still gone. He was never coming back.

I walked closer to the hole as they lowered his body into the ground. I know people thought I was probably going to dive in like I wanted to, but instead, I threw a straw into the hole. It was a straw I used to get high with. I refused to let my baby die in vain. I vowed to stay clean because I knew he would always be smiling down on me.

I looked at Sarita carrying on; for real, I wanted to smack the shit out of her for what she said, but I knew this was not the time or place. Plus, how I felt, I probably would have killed that girl. But I had to take my hurt out on somebody. I could tell that Seth was well loved by the crowd that showed up for him today.

I thought it was nice of his mom to make sure they put my name in the obituary as the lady in his life. The funeral was comical because many females wanted to be relevant. Suddenly, they came from everywhere, talking about what Seth meant to them. I'm glad I'm confident in who I am because I didn't pay any attention to them.

I looked over at Keena, and she had that pregnancy glow. In a way, I wished I were pregnant too so I could still have a piece of Seth to hold on to. I know it would be hard for anybody to replace Seth. He showed me what real love is supposed to be like.

Keena

I wasn't that close to Seth, but I loved him because of Kim and Peter's love for him. We were getting close because of the relationships that surrounded us. I shed a few tears, but they were nothing compared to what Peter and Kim shed. My heart goes out to Kim. I don't know how I could handle this if the shoe were on the other foot and we were burying Peter, not Seth. I knew how much Kim loved Seth. He overlooked her flaws and helped her to get clean. When she needed him the most, he was there. Any other nigga would have turned their back on her without hearing her story. Seth knew she wanted better in life, and he stood there to ensure she did better.

I didn't know how to comfort Peter. Kim was right there. I could pick up the phone and call her or see her. Peter could no longer do that with Seth. I was trying to be there for both of them. I knew they both needed me. I self-consciously rubbed my belly while looking over at Sarita's dumb ass. She disgusted me, and she better be glad I had enough respect for Ms. Pam to stand down. I can't take that bitch seriously. I can't believe she had the nerve to talk about a baby that she aborted. But she wanted to be relevant, I guess.

I heard Paulina yell out how she would miss her brother. In all the madness, nobody thought about her feelings. Seth had been around her whole life, and he was all she knew too. My heart went out to her as well.

I grabbed Kim's hand on my left and Peter's on my right. I was in the middle of my two favorite people in the world. I knew they both needed me right now. I wouldn't have it any other way. As I stepped back into the limo, I blew a kiss toward Seth's grave, and it seemed as if the wind had just started blowing the trees out of nowhere. I took that as a sign from Seth that everything would be all right.

"Did you see how that wind just came out of nowhere?" Peter asked me as he got into the car behind me.

"I did."

"That was my nigga still letting us feel his presence." Peter let out a light chuckle as he closed the door.

Getting over that hump was the hard part. We appreciate everyone that came out, but after today, Seth will be a distant memory to all the people, but his close friends and family will forever have an aching hole in their hearts.

Epilogue

"Push, Keena. Come on, baby, you can do it."

I looked over at Peter as he tried to coach me to push our baby out, but I was exhausted. I had been in labor for seventeen hours, and it seemed like my baby would never come. Kim was standing at the head of my bed, wiping beads of sweat off my forehead. Then she whispered in my ear that I could do this.

I didn't want them to know, but I was scared as hell. My blood pressure was already out of control, and the nurses and doctors kept talking about how I could have a stroke and die if my blood pressure didn't stabilize. I also didn't know what kind of mother I would be since I had never had a mother figure. I didn't have a woman to show me the way. So I pretty much had to figure everything out for myself.

"Come on, Keena. Another contraction is coming. On three, I need you to push hard." This was the nurse talking this time. I was ready for this to be over, so I pushed with everything I had.

"I see the head, Keena. I see the head. Come on and push. I'm ready to meet my baby."

The sound of Peter's voice saying he saw our baby's head gave me motivation, so I gave it one more big push. That one push must have worked because the next thing I knew, the doctor yelled out it was a boy weighing nine pounds, ten ounces, and twenty-one inches long.

Peter was raining kisses all over my face. I knew he was happy to meet our son. I looked at the huge rock on my hand and then looked down at my son. My life was now complete. We had a destination wedding in the sixth month of my pregnancy. Peter said he didn't want to bring our son into this world with us not being married. But honestly, it didn't matter to me. If Peter were in my life, I would be happy.

Seth's middle name was Lamontay, and we named our baby that in his memory. Ms. Pam thanked us for that because it made her happy. Ms. Pam ended up moving back to Miami. Kim asked her to share Seth's house with her. Ms. Pam is like a mother to Kim, and they have the best relationship. Ms. Pam even gave Kim the greenlight if she started dating someone again. She told her she was young, and there was no way she expected her not to move on.

Kim walked around here like a zombie for a few months. At one time, I thought she had started back using, but she assured me that was not the case. I had no other choice than to believe her. Eventually, I am sure Kim will start dating again, but right now, it is too soon. They say time heals all wounds so that she will heal one day but in her own time. You cannot tell people how long they are supposed to grieve. It has been thirteen years, and I still miss my dad, and I'm sure I always will.

Peter was no longer in the streets. He gave it all up the day he buried his best friend. He said he had to be around to raise our baby, and he didn't want to go out like Seth. We had plenty of money from both of our investments. Neither of us ever had to work a day of our lives again. We made an agreement that this fast life was not worth our sanity.

I came to Miami on a mission. This was supposed to be a temporary stay, but I ended up with a husband and a